IMPULS

The Companion to PULSE

New York Times & USA Today Bestselling Author
Deborah Bladon

Copyright

First Original Print Edition, October 2014
Copyright © 2014 by Deborah Bladon
ISBN-13: 978-1502804006
ISBN-10: 150280400X

Cover Design by Wolf & Eagle Media.

Also by Deborah Bladon

The Obsessed Series
The Exposed Series
The Pulse Series
The VAIN Series
The RUIN Series
SOLO

Chapter 1

"Mr. Moore? Ms. Ross is here to see you."

I chuckle as I pull myself out of my uncomfortable leather office chair after ending the call with my secretary. I glance at the clock on the wall above my desk. Two o'clock. Jessica's late. She's very late. She promised to stop by between classes before lunch.

"She did it again, Nathan." Her lips brush over mine, almost thoughtlessly, as she pushes past me into my office. "My name is Roth, not Ross. She'll never get it right."

"Jessica, I told you she has a lisp." I slam the door shut with my foot before I reach for her elbow. "You're late."

"School is a bitch right now." She subtly tries to break free of my grasp but there's no conviction behind the movement. "Remind me why I wanted to be a chef."

I pull her back into my chest, enveloping her body in my arms. I relish in the feeling of the soft fabric of the wrap dress she's wearing. "It's your dream. You're going to open your own restaurant one day."

"I can't afford that." She shakes her head. "I'm not sure I even want it anymore."

I look down to where her delicate hands are covering my own. The contrast is striking. She's always said that she feels small next to me. I love protecting her. Pleasing her and taking care of her is my life's mission now. "You want it, Jessica." I reach down to run my lips over her ear. "You aren't going to give up. You're not a quitter."

She spins around quickly on her heel, her hands darting to my neck. I have little time to respond before her lush, soft lips are on mine. My hands drop to her ass, cupping it in my palms, pulling her body towards me. I'm stiff, hard and ready for her already. I always am. The moment she touches me, all resistance I may have felt vanishes. This is the one and only woman I've ever met that I can't live without. There is nothing she can ask of me that I won't willingly and eagerly do for her. I'm pussy whipped. We both know it.

"Did you come here so I could fuck you?" I trace my lips along the soft curve of her chin. "You ran off when I was in the shower this morning. I wanted to taste you before I left for the office."

She moans into my hair. I know she's wet. She's always wet when I tell her how badly my body aches for hers. I move my hands up her thighs, skimming the hem of the dress, pulling it up as I go. The way she glides her tongue over her bottom lip only incites me further. I pull on the edge of her silk panties, feeling the heat of her arousal before my fingers slide over the smooth folds.

"Tonight I'll suck your..." The words tumble out of her perfect lips wrapped in a low moan. "Nathan," she says my name just as I push one finger inside of her. "Nathan, please."

"I can make you come just like this," I growl. There's no arrogance in the statement at all. It's the truth. I can touch Jessica in a way that will throw her into the deepest clutches of an intense orgasm just by using my hand. I did it the first night we met, and I've been perfecting my technique at every single opportunity since then.

"Do it," she purrs into my shoulder. "Now."

I don't need any encouragement. My body is driving my need to hear the soft whimpers that flow out of the deepest parts of her when she gives herself to me. I skim my index finger over her clit, circling the small, swollen bud before dipping two fingers into her tight, wet channel.

"Nathan." My name is barely more than a whispered whimper. Her breathing shifts and her hands grab tightly to my shoulders. "I'm going to..."

"You're going to fucking come all over my hand, Jessica," I interrupt. "Then I'm going to lick every one of my fingers clean."

Her body tenses as I push my fingers farther into her. "Oh, God, please."

I pull back just enough to watch her beautiful face as she loses control against me. Her entire body shudders. Her knees weaken and she falls into my chest. My hand continues pushing, pulling and kneading every ounce of pleasure out of her until she stills against me.

"You're so fucking hot." My brow rises as her long lashes flutter. It takes another moment before she slowly opens her big, beautiful blue eyes.

"I didn't come here for that." The words are meant to sound robust but the heavy breaths she's pulling in transform them into something seductive, too seductive. My cock is still hard, wanting and needing to be inside of her.

I spin her around almost effortlessly until her back is against my office door. My fingers fall to the zipper of my pants. "I'm going to fuck you, Jessica. That's what you came here for."

"Oh, shit." Her eyes widen as her gaze falls to my hand and my thick, heavy dick resting in my palm.

I smile at the expression on her face. There's no mistaking she wants me as much as I want her. I've fucked her beautiful body almost every day since she moved into my apartment a year ago. My body feels bereft the moment I come inside of her. The want never ceases. The desire to consume her never quiets. I can't get enough of her.

I don't hesitate as I pull her panties to the side before I drive my cock into her in one fluid movement. My hand jumps to her chin, tilting her head to the side so I can capture her scream in my kiss. I push my tongue into her mouth and claim it; the very same way my body is claiming hers. My free hand moves to her leg, hitching it up as I pound into her, each stroke deeper than the last. She tries to speak. I know that she's going to tell me that people outside the office will know. They'll hear us. I don't fucking care.

Her hands settle in my hair, pulling on the black locks. She knows I love that exquisite bite of pain as I near my release. I pound faster and harder. I'm like a man who has been starved of food for weeks. The truth is that I fucked her last night before I went to sleep. I bent her over the bed and rammed myself into her until I came all over her beautiful ass.

"Jessica, fuck you're so good. Come for me." I can't control the words or the feelings when it's like this. She's a part of me when I'm this close and all I want and need is to hear her come.

She yanks on my hair, pulling my head back as my name falls from her mouth over and over again. Her sex clenches around me and I lose all sense of space and time. I can only feel and as I empty myself into her, I lunge forward, pressing her body into me, soaking in the fragrance of her skin, the scent of her breath and the feeling of her body taking every last drop.

"Nathan, I…"

I don't let her speak. I run my lips over hers, diving into her mouth with my tongue. "Goddamn, that was amazing," I growl into her neck. "That was worth waiting for."

She pulls back and my cock falls from her body. I tuck it back into my pants before reaching behind me to grab a tissue from the holder on my desk. I kneel down and carefully pull the tissue between her folds.

I feel her hand graze through my hair before it settles on my cheek. "I didn't come here for that, Nathan." There's absolutely no denying the amusement woven into her words. "I came because you asked me to."

I bolt to my feet, shooting the tissue towards the wastebasket that is at full capacity. I watch in silence as it rolls off the rim of a paper coffee cup before falling to the floor. "I have to tell you something," I say before looking at her. I've been avoiding telling her this for the past two weeks. It's not because I think she'll take the news badly. She won't. Jessica is my biggest supporter. She's the one who constantly tells me what a great attorney I am. Most people would think they were empty words given the fact that she has little grasp on what I actually do. Being a securities attorney doesn't afford me the same high profile excitement that a prosecutor or defense attorney bathes in. For the most part, my job is lackluster. It consists of mostly long hours and boring meetings. I love it though, and I love that Jessica is proud of me.

"What?" She adjusts the hemline of her dress before her hands dart to her long, blonde hair.

I push her hands away, pulling on the strands, straightening it over her shoulders. "It's about my work."

Her eyes dart to my desk that is covered with folders, papers and half empty paper cups. "What about it?"

I run my finger along her jaw, savoring the feeling of the softness of her skin. Her pink lips part slightly before her top teeth come into view. Her tongue darts out and pulls a lazy path over her lips. Christ. How the fuck am I supposed to talk business when I'm staring at that?

"Nathan." Her voice pulls me back to reality. "You're making me nervous. What is it?"

"I want you to understand something first." I motion to one of the two office chairs that sit in front of my desk. "Sit down, Jessica."

She acquiesces and crosses her legs. Her hands pull together in a nervous huddle on her lap. "Just say it."

I scan her face, noting how knotted her brow looks. She's worried. It's the same expression she had on her face three months ago when I told her that I was considering moving back to Boston to accept a position at a firm there. It was a fleeting fantasy that would give me more time with my sister and her kids. I hadn't considered it seriously because I know that Jessica's life is here now. After being accepted into culinary school, any career plans I may have seem trivial compared to hers. Cooking is her passion. Being a lawyer is my job. My passion is her.

"Do we have to move?" Her voice cracks only slightly with the question. "Where do you want us to move to now?"

The question bites through me but not because of the obvious disappointment that is woven into each of the words, but because she's willing. I slip my suit jacket off before lowering myself into the chair next to her. I reach for her hands, pulling them into my own. "We're not moving anywhere."

I see the relief leave her shoulders and face. She holds tightly to my hands. "Tell me, Nathan. Please tell me."

The sound of my name on her lips pushes me forward. No one says it the way Jessica does. I've never told her but I sometimes deliberately let her calls go to voicemail so I can listen to her saying my name in the messages she leaves me. "I'm being considered for partner."

Her body stalls and her mouth falls open slightly. It's distracting, way too fucking distracting for me to continue. How the hell am I supposed to talk about the vetting process now? Christ, I wish I had asked her to suck me off this morning.

"Partner?" Her bottom lips juts out. It's not helping. It's only reminding me how she pulls her lips slowly over the head of my dick as she strokes the length with her hands. "You mean it will be Avery, Davidson and Moore?"

It's the first time I've heard anyone say it other than myself. I only nod in response, watching the way her eyes are darting from my face to my desk.

"Nathan, I'm so…" She moves her body to the edge of her chair. Her hands jump to my shoulders. She closes her eyes and swallows hard.

"Jessica," I say her name slowly and deliberately, wanting to pull her back from wherever her mind has wandered. I need her to understand that it won't change anything between us. "It's not a done deal yet."

Her eyes open slowly and I'm instantly pulled into them. I watch as a tear falls down her cheek, pulling with it a faint line of black mascara.

"What's wrong?" My thumb darts to curb the tear, drawing it into my flesh. "Jessica, tell me."

"I'm so proud of you, Nathan." A small smile pulls at the corner of her mouth. "I'm so proud of you."

Chapter 2

"When will they make a decision?" Her tone is just as giddy as it was when I first told her about the potential partnership ten minutes ago. "I'm so excited."

"In a few weeks." I tug my thumb over her lip. "They're considering a few of the other attorneys for it too."

"Why?" Her brows pop up with the question. "Who could be better than you?"

I love her exuberance. I love that she sees the best in me now. The beginning of our relationship was a twisted maze of confusion. All of my past one night stands had clouded Jessica's perception of me. I'd worked hard to prove to her that I was honorable, good and completely in love with her. We're in a great place now and seeing how thrilled she is at my news only solidifies my need to get her to marry me.

"Marry me." I toss the words out so nonchalantly that her head almost snaps back.

"You didn't just say that." Her hands bolt to the arms of the chair. "Tell me you didn't just ask me to marry you again."

"I did," I say sheepishly. "I told you I'd ask you every day until you said yes."

"Nathan." Her tone is even and unreadable. "That's not romantic."

It's a weak argument but it's enough to move the conversation away from the one subject she's always avoiding. "I'll take that as a no?" I push my luck.

"When will you find out about the partnership?" Her eyes bore into me. "Will you tell me as soon as you know?"

I nod, soaking in the wide grin on her face. "We have to talk about something else too. I didn't ask you to come down here just to tell you about my work."

She scans my face quickly and I see the veil of disappointment that hovers beneath her gaze. "What is it?" The question seems genuine but we both know it's just a courtesy. She knows what I'm about to bring up. It's a topic she's been hedging around skillfully for weeks. Time is running out though and I need to press this. Not just for her, but for me too.

"It's about the wedding." I tap my finger over the tip of your nose. "Your sister emailed me again last night. She needs an answer, Jessica."

Her cheeks go sallow as she hears the words. "I told you I didn't want to go, Nathan."

I've never met Jessica's family. I've loved this woman for more than a year and I've never had the opportunity to go to Connecticut to see the people who loved and nurtured her as she was growing into who she is today. I've listened to her talk with her sister. I've held her hand as she's given shattered glimpses into the pain of her parent's divorce and I sat idly by as she told her father that he couldn't come to visit her over the holidays because of her work schedule. She won't share. I won't pry but this wedding is a ticket to her past, and I want to be aboard that train.

"Your sister really wants you to be her maid of honor, Jessica," I say gently. I've tried coaxing, being overbearing and manipulative. Today's approach is compassionate guilt. I'm hoping this will be the one thing that finally works.

"Julie has a lot of friends." Her hands drop into her lap. "They don't need me there."

I inch forward on my chair, pulling on the fabric of my pants to give me the room to maneuver myself closer to her. "I'll be right beside you the entire time. I won't leave your side for a second."

"What if Josh is there?"

I feel the vein in my neck pulse at the sound of her ex-boyfriend's name. This is the guy that calls her like clockwork every few months, trying to weasel his way back into her life. She knows exactly how to handle him. She wields masterful control over him on the phone like a professional lion tamer. I have to admit, the thought of seeing them together in a room isn't doing anything for my temper. I can't stand the thought of any man being close to her. The idea of her talking face-to-face with a guy she used to fuck is sending my stomach reeling.

"He's friends with Julie. You know that he is." She's almost pleading. I can hear her trying to make a new case for not attending the wedding. I'm not about to let her off the hook that easily though.

"Your sister wants you there." I run my hand over her exposed calf. "Julie loves you. She's your only sister, Jessica. This is the most important day of her life."

"What about Josh?" She pushes, knowing that his name scorches over me like hot coals.

I'm not giving in this time. After reading the email her sister sent me last night, I am bound and determined to get Jessica's pretty little ass to Connecticut. "Fuck him. It's not about him."

Her expression goes blank. "I don't want to go, Nathan. I don't."

"You're going to regret not going." I sigh. We've been dancing around the subject for more than a month. She has to make a firm decision now so her sister can choose someone else to be her maid of honor if Jessica can't get her shit together enough to get her ass on a plane. "Do it for her."

Her mouth falls open and I half-expect a litany of curse words to fly out at me. She snaps it shut before she finally speaks. "Okay, I'll go. But you can't leave my side."

"Never, Jessica." I graze my lips over hers. "I'll never leave your side."

Chapter 3

"So this is him?" Her breath races over my face and I'm immediately assaulted with the unpleasant combination of a cheap domestic beer and even cheaper cigarettes. "Jessie, why didn't you tell me he was such a stud?"

Jessica's face flashes crimson as she grabs tightly to my hand. "I sent you a picture of us, mom."

"He didn't look this dashing in that picture." Her hand grazes over my forearm right before I sense her fingers trailing down my dress shirt towards my ass.

I edge to the left, pulling Jessica into my body. "We should get to the hotel." The effort to avoid her mother's wandering hand does little good as I feel her grab a handful of my ass through my dress pants. Christ. She's not even trying to hide it. We're standing in a room filled with Jessica's relatives and her mother's making a beeline for my goods.

"Good idea." Jessica's expression is pained. I can see the discomfort there. I feel a brief sense of regret knowing that I'm the one who incessantly pushed her to come to this wedding. We arrived at her mother's house less than five minutes ago and I already wish we were back in our apartment in Manhattan.

"That's nuts," Hillary, Jessica's mother, practically spits all over me as the words fly off her lips. "I have lots of extra space. You two should stay here."

The vise grip that Jessica has on my hand only tightens. I don't need to look at her to know that staying here isn't an option. Hell, it's not an option for me either. I can only imagine what will happen to me if I wander down to the kitchen at night to get a sandwich. Hillary has made it clear by the continued groping of my ass that she wants whatever the fuck she can get from me.

"Mom, I don't think that's a good idea," she says in a sweet voice. No one in the room, including her grandmother can hear the veiled disgust woven into the words. Why didn't I listen when she said she didn't want to come back here? I feel as though I've stepped into a circus and my ass is the main attraction.

"Nonsense." The word is a slur. "I can fix up your old room. My sewing machine is in there now but your strong fellow can cart that out of there. I bet he has huge muscles."

Jessica tosses me a dazed look. "Nathan already booked the hotel. We're more comfortable there."

"She's right," I yelp. This time Hillary's finger got closer than the urologist during my prostate exam. "I'm tired. We're going to the hotel."

"You're coming to the rehearsal dinner, aren't you, Jess?" Julie, Jessica's sister, pokes her head around a corner and into the room. At first glance you'd never know the two of them were sisters. Julie's dark hair and eyes pair flawlessly with her olive toned skin. She's the exact physical opposite of Jessica. She hovers near my height and her body is elegantly toned and trim.

"I'll…we'll be there." Jessica looks to me for reassurance.

I slide my hand to her neck, pulling her head into my chest. "We will both be there."

"I can't wait," Hillary hisses into my ear.

***

"Nathan, I can't," she whimpers into the rough sheets on the bed. "I can't do it again."

I race my tongue over her folds again. "You need to come again, Jessica. I need it."

She pushes back and I suck her swollen bud between my lips, grazing my teeth over it. I grab tightly to her thighs, pulling them even further apart. I'm rewarded with a soft moan. I can tell by the way her body is moving that she's close again already. The moment we checked into the hotel and dropped our bags on the floor, I pulled her clothes off, made her get on all fours and my face dove between her legs. I wanted to taste her. I wanted to hear the beautiful sound of her coming under my tongue and touch. Seeing her so vulnerable and exposed is all the reward I need.

Her back arches as the orgasm floods through her. I lean back to watch the fluid movement of her body as it's overcome with pleasure. Her legs collapse, her ass wiggles and her hands grasp firmly to the sheets, pulling them loose from the mattress. My name

flutters into the stillness of the air over and over again as she falls
back down from the edge of her desire.

"Nathan, fuck me." It's a half whisper, barely audible. My
heart is pounding heavily from watching her body reacting to my
touch. "Fuck me hard."

I bolt to my knees, pulling open my pants and freeing my
cock. I don't waste a moment before I push it into her, slowly at first.
She's so wet, but it's still so much for her. It's always been so much
and the exquisite tightness almost pushes me into a deep orgasm
immediately. I have to pull back slightly to temper what I'm feeling.

She glances back, her hair flying over her face. The moisture
settling on her top lip only makes her that much more seductive. It's
not surprising that I couldn't control myself the first moment I laid
eyes on her at the club in Manhattan. I wanted all of her then and
nothing has changed. I'm consumed with my need for her.

"Fuck, this is so good," I hiss through clenched teeth. I still
while I undo my cuff links. I toss them on the bed. I slide the blue
dress shirt off my shoulders before grabbing heavily to her hips.

"I love when you fuck me hard." She's a temptress and she
knows it. The words she uses when I'm buried balls deep in her body
push me into a place I've never been before. I've fucked hundreds of
women but this is the only woman I've ever made love to. I need to
feel her come again before I can release. I have to. My body won't
allow anything else.

I rail back on my heels and pull tightly to her hips as I ram
my dick relentlessly into her. "Christ, you're so fucking tight,
Jessica. I'll never get used to it."

"Harder, Nathan." She pushes back against me, her wetness
enveloping my cock like a slick, taut glove. She raises her body,
pushing her hands into the mattress to give herself more flexibility.

I take on the challenge, plunging myself further and further
into her. "Goddamn," I scream. "I'm going to shoot my load in you.
It's going to fill you up."

That's enough to throw her over the edge. She cries out as her
muscles tense around my cock, pushing me into the middle of an
intense and overwhelming orgasm.

"Christ, shit. Jessica," I call out from the sheer weight of the
pleasure coursing through each and every one of my cells. "I fucking
can't believe it." I can't. It's so good. It's only gotten better and better.

We know each other's bodies so well. She knows how to make me come so hard.

"Nathan," she whispers my name only the way she can. "I loved that."

"I love you." I curl up next to her, pulling her warm, nude body into my chest. "I fucking love you."

Chapter 4

"Your tits are way too big for that dress."

"I know," she throws the words at me as she stares at herself in the full length mirror on the back of the closet door. "I sent my sister the measurements but I feel like I'm going to have a nipple slip."

"I don't mind," I tease. Truth is I do mind. If that piece of shit ex-boyfriend of hers is at this wedding he's going to be drooling all over Jessica in that sad excuse of a dress her sister ordered for her. "Maybe your dress is mixed up with one of the bridesmaids."

"They're wearing a different color." She shrugs at her own reflection in the mirror as she hikes up the front of the strapless, navy blue, floor length dress yet again. "I look ridiculous."

She doesn't. She looks fucking breathtaking. She's pulled her hair up into a messy bun on the top of her head. She's wearing minimal make up and her hourglass figure is on full display in the dress. I can't fathom why her sister chose this dress for her. Any man in the church is going to fall to his knees and praise the heavens for this vision. "You look beautiful." I toss her a cheesy smile as I watch her tenderly try to fasten the clasp on the necklace I bought her for her birthday a few months ago. The chain is delicate, the single sapphire stone in the center of the silver pendant a constant reminder of the color of her eyes. I had my friend, Ivy, design it in her studio just for Jessica. She wears it almost daily and each time I see it around her neck, I'm in awe of how its beauty only adds to her own.

"Help me, please." She smiles at my reflection in the mirror. "I only need your help with the necklace. Don't touch the dress."

I throw my head back in laughter. The first time she asked me to zip her up this afternoon I pushed the dress down and pinched her nipples while she rubbed her hand over her wetness until she came in the mirror for me. This time I'll try and behave. "I won't touch the dress." I pitch my hands in the air in playful surrender. "I'll help with the necklace and then we'll go."

She nods as her eyes stare into mine in the mirror. "You're so handsome, Nathan."

I pull my gaze away from hers. I do it as much to focus on the small clasp of the necklace as to regain my composure. She sees into the deepest parts of me. She knows me better than anyone ever has and she still adores me, flaws and all. It's moments like this when I question whether I'm good enough for her. She's perfection and innocence woven into the most beautiful creature I've ever seen. I'm jaded, used and cynical. I can't help but wonder what I've done in this lifetime to deserve this much happiness.

"Nathan?" Her soft voice calls to me as I stare at the clasp. My fingers are still inches apart. I haven't moved since she told me how handsome she thinks I am. "Is it broken?"

"No." I fasten it before adjusting the chain around her neck. "It's perfect, Jessica. Just like you."

***

"Have you ever fucked in the backseat of a Cadillac?" A woman's voice assaults me from the right.

I feel as though I've been transported back to my teenage years. Judging by the reception hall and the outfits of the majority of the guests, I'd say I'm right on target with that estimation. Now, I'm being propositioned by a woman who looks like a librarian, knee high wool socks and all.

"Did you hear me, gorgeous?" She steps closer and I inch back towards the makeshift wooden bar.

"I'll have a bourbon neat, and …"

"I'll have a Bloody Mary." She interrupts me with a wink and I literally shudder. I stare over her shoulder to where Jessica is huddled in a group with her sister and the bridesmaids. I smile to myself as I watch her pull on the top of the dress, trying to keep her breasts where they belong. My eyes dart across the room to Josh Redmond, her ex-boyfriend. He's sitting at his table, his eyes honed in on the woman I'll be crawling into bed with later tonight.

"Thanks for buying me a drink." The librarian leans closer still. I'm trapped between her and a wall.

I stare down at her briefly. "The drinks are free."

"You're not from here, are you?" Her hand leaps to my lapel. "Your suit is real nice."

I want to reach up and swat her hand away but I have no idea who she is. For all I know she's one of Jessica's oldest and dearest friends. That's hard to imagine, given the fact she doesn't talk about anyone she left behind when she ran away from here to Manhattan.

"Where are you from?" she asks as she presses her body into mine.

I lurch my hips back quickly trying to meld into the plaster which covers all the walls in this school gymnasium. As much as Jessica's sister and her husband wish it looked like a reception hall, it doesn't. The basketball hoops on the opposite ends of the room can't be disguised, even though it appears that someone tried to hide them beneath a mile of colorful streamers. "Manhattan," I offer. The less details the better. This conversation is going nowhere quickly.

"Have you ever had a one night stand?"

I almost spit the entire mouthful of bourbon I just gulped on her plain yellow dress. Have I ever had a one night stand? Jesus. This woman has no idea who she's talking to. "Why?" I bark back. My sex life is none of her business.

"I'm horny."

It's a declaration I should have seen coming like a freight train on a runaway track. The way she's shifting back and forth on her brown heels is enough of a clue that the woman's crotch is on fire. Even if Jessica wasn't in the picture, I'd turn this one down. Something tells me she'd eat me alive before we even got to the parking lot.

"Keep your panties on." I tip my drink in her direction. "I'm taken."

"By who?" She dips her chin and raises a brow, challenging me to answer.

"Jessica Roth," I counter. "She's that beautiful blonde over there."

She turns sharply in Jessica's direction. We both gawk as we watch her run her hands over the front of her ill fitted dress. Her left hand stops briefly as she subtly traces a slow path over her left breast with her index finger.

"Wow." The librarian pulls in a heavy breath. "She's even hotter now."

I stare at Jessica as she blows me a kiss across the room. Normally, a sticky sweet gesture like that would be a turn off, but seeing her lips pursed together like that makes my cock jump to life.

I have to pull in a steely breath before the librarian notices it. "You know her?" I ask, hoping it will keep her gaze on my face and not on my groin.

"We went to high school together." Her eyes dart down to my pants and I swear I see her tongue smooth a path over her bottom lip. "I'm Charity."

The name doesn't suit her in the least. "Nathan," I offer back before finishing the plastic glass of bourbon the bartender offered me. "Another?" I place it down and nod at him.

He murmurs something under his breath before he refills the glass to the half-way point.

"You two are dating?" She pulls her hand through her short brown hair.

I take a small sip of the liquid, grateful for the slight buzz I'm starting to feel. I haven't eaten anything since this morning and judging by the lack of any food on the banquet tables, I'd say dinner is hours away yet. "We live together."

"You're her rebound?"

The question bites and I get the unmistakable impression that's its intention. Why wouldn't it sting? Virtually every person in this room knows Jessica as the other half of Josh. Even their names belong together. Why the fuck did I keep insisting we come to this wedding? I could be back in my apartment buried in Jessica's body hearing her scream my name and my name only.

"I'm not her rebound." I don't want to sound as angry as I do." Jessica loves me. She never loved Josh the way she loves me."

Her eyes dash to Jessica before they settle back on me." I wasn't talking about Josh," she chuckles." I'm talking about him." She stops there, right fucking there before adding anything else.

I stare at her wishing I knew what the hell she was talking about. Who the fuck is she referring to? I know Jessica's had three lovers. She told me. I practically fucked it out of her months and months ago. I had to know. My imagination couldn't shut up until I knew how many men had been inside of her. I just assumed that Josh was the most important one. He's the only one she ever talked about. They were together for years before she bolted from Bloomfield, Connecticut and landed in New York City.

Charity can't shut the hell up. "You have no idea who I'm talking about do you?" Her tone is peevish.

I stare at Jessica across the room. I watch a few wayward hairs fall out of the bun and onto her shoulders. I look at her body. It's so beautiful. It's soft, supple, and made for fucking. For the first time since I fell in love with her, I feel entirely in the dark. There's no way in hell I'm letting the librarian have the satisfaction of knowing that I don't have a fucking clue about who she's talking about. I can't believe I've never heard Jessica talk about either of the other two guys she's slept with. Why didn't I press for more? Why did I drop it?

"Charity, as fetching as his conversation has been I need to go see my girl." I slam my now empty glass down on the bar. The motion causes the bar to teeter back and forth slightly. I push past her trying to maneuver around her.

She steps into my path almost tripping over her own shoes. It's obvious she's a lightweight. She can't even handle half of a Bloody Mary. I reach to grab her elbow helping to level her steps. My mind is racing, my heart is pounding and all I can hear over and over in my mind is the word *him*.

"None of us thought that Jessica would ever get over the senator," she whispers." It would take someone like you to make that happen."

The senator? The fucking senator? What the hell has Jessica been hiding from me? I close my eyes briefly trying to wash away the image of a teenage Jessica with a man old enough to be a senator. It doesn't work. I rummage through my memory grasping for anything she may have said to me about a man who worked for the government. Why the fuck didn't she tell me about this?

"How long have you been with her?" Charity isn't one to give up easily. Did she hook up with you right after she moved?"

The question feels like a sharp slap across my cheek. Jessica was at that club two weeks after she moved from Connecticut to Manhattan. She told me all she wanted was a random fuck. I thought it was all just for fun the night I met her. Then I thought it was because she was running away from Josh. Maybe the entire time she's been running away from the man that she loves. Maybe that's why she can't say yes whenever I ask her to marry me.

Chapter 5

"I'm so glad that's over," she says softly. "Josh didn't even try to talk to me once."

I lean against the wall of the elevator my eyes glued to her face. "He knew I'd deck him if he did." I playfully curl my hands into fists as I take on a boxer's stance.

Her hand darts to cover her mouth as she giggles. I knew the moment I danced with her that she had too much champagne. "You're my knight in shining armor. You'll always take care of me, Nathan. Won't you?"

The words stab through me like a hot spear. "I would do anything for you Jessica. Anything," I say without any hesitation. It's true. I would do anything she asked of me.

She stares at me across the elevator as it makes its way slowly to the twenty-second floor of the only hotel that had any available rooms. "Will you let me suck your cock?" She pulls her tongue over her top lip as the words fill the small space. Her hands slide up from her waist to the top of the dress. She slowly, deliberately, and seductively pulls it down revealing her round, full breasts.

"Christ, Jessica," I growl at her. "What if someone gets on?"

She takes small steps across the elevator until she's standing directly in front of me. "I guess they'll get to watch." Her hands jump to my waist. Her lips trail a path across my chin. "I've been thinking about the taste of you all night."

The lift jars to a sudden stop on our floor. I quickly slide my suit jacket off my shoulders and wrap it around her body. "I'm going to come so hard in your mouth, Jessica." I pull her into me as the door flies open. "I'm going to give you everything you need."

She's on me the moment I push open the hotel room door. I have no time to react. Her dress is on the floor. Her panties are right behind. She stands in front of me completely naked and exposed save for the nude heels she's wearing. "Take off your pants, Nathan."

"Do it yourself, Jessica." I nod towards the carpeted floor. "Get on your knees and slide my cock into your mouth. Suck on it hard. Make it good. Make me come."

She drops to her knees without an ounce of indecision. "Talk to me, Nathan. Tell me what you want."

I don't resist as she unbuckles my pants and slides the zipper down. I lean back against the wall looking down at her. "Roll your tongue over the head. Slide your hands around it."

"I love this. Your cock is beautiful." Her full lips graze over the head before she pulls it entirely into her mouth.

"Fuck." The word escapes from deep within me. I can't control it. I've been sucked off by so many women whose names I can't even remember. None of them came close to comparing to her. Not one of them made me feel the way that Jessica does. "Cup my balls in your hand. Squeeze them, Jessica."

She moans around the heavy root. "Nathan, it's so good."

"So good," I say through clenched teeth. My hands drop to her head. I wind my fingers through her hair, releasing the bun. I pull sharply on the strands, helping her find her rhythm. I fuck her mouth slowly and rhythmically.

She adjusts herself on the floor. Her hands circle my cock as they glide up and down, pulling my desire from deep within my core.

"I'm going to fucking come down your throat, Jessica," I hiss. "You're going to swallow every last drop."

"Do it," she challenges. "Give it all to me, Nathan."

That's all the encouragement I need. I jerk my hips forward and yank on her hair as I feel the first rush of my desire shoot into her mouth. "God damn you, Jessica. Fuck me."

***

"Will you brush my hair for me?" She steps out of the steam filled washroom, the only towel covering her, wrapped tightly around her head. "I love when you do that for me."

I help her into one of the terry cloth robes I found hanging in the closet of our deluxe suite. She watches in silence as I roll up the arms and adjust the belt. It's obvious that the robe was designed for someone twice her size. "I'll get your hairbrush." I kiss her gently on her forehead. "You sit there, on the edge of the bed."

I don't look back as I turn into the washroom. I switch on the fan. The loud whir coming from it another indication of the age of the building. The torn and faded green wallpaper that drapes the area behind the mirror is damp from the steam. I race my hand over the mirror, staring at my reflection. I need to ask her. I've barely said two words to her since she blew me. She wanted me to take a shower with her but I couldn't. My mind kept imagining her down on her knees, with some faceless senator's cock stuffed down her throat. I have to clear the images away. I need to understand what he meant to her, and if her reluctance to commit to me is because she's still bound to him in her heart.

"Nathan?" Her soft voice carries through the doorway. "Did I forget to pack it?"

It? The fucking hairbrush. I rummage through the tote she packed all her products in. I wiggle my hand down to the bottom and pull out the hairbrush. "I've got it."

"I'm glad we can go home tomorrow," she says the moment I step back into the room. The towel is strewn across the bed now. Her wet, long blonde hair clings to her face. The imperfection of the strands only adds to her beauty. When she's like this, natural and exposed, I feel as though there's nothing that can ever come between us. She knows the worst in me and still looks at me with more love in her eyes than I ever knew existed. Now, I have to break open something that she's buried within her. I keep telling myself that if the senator was an important part of her life that she would have brought him up. Honestly, she never talks about her past. It's always been a mystery to me.

I pull the brush tenderly through her hair, working through the small knots in silence. Her breathing is slow, strong and calm. She moves slightly each time the brush gets caught.

"Are you okay?" she asks softly.

It's the question I knew was coming. I don't lie to Jessica. I've skirted around the truth in the past and it's always been a disaster. She expects utter and complete honesty from me and I want to give that to her. I need to. I can't let this fester inside of me anymore. It's fucking driving me crazy imagining every possible scenario there is. I need to ask her about the senator so she can tell me it was a forgettable blip in her past. I want her to tell me that she can't even remember his name.

Her head dips slightly forward and the brush tangles in a strand. Her hand instinctively darts to the spot. "That hurt, Nathan."

I don't want her to say my name right now. It makes me weak. I can't feel weak for this. "I'm sorry." The words are meant to sound more genuine than they do. "I'll be more careful."

She pulls her feet onto the bed, circling her arms around her knees. ""Something's bothering you. No secrets, remember?"

The words tear through me. I'm not the one with the secret. It's her. "No secrets," I repeat in a barely audible tone. "I don't want there to be secrets."

Her breathing stalls. I watch her shoulders tense beneath the thin fabric of the robe. "Do you have a secret?" The question is calm and sensitive. She's not jumping up to her feet or to any conclusions at all. She's grown in trust. She knows my life is hers and that everything is an open book.

"You do," I say without thought. This isn't how I wanted the conversation to go. I didn't want to throw this at her from left field before she was ready to catch it. I'm giving her little time to prepare. It's a tactic I use constantly in the courtroom, but Jessica isn't on trial. I have to stop assuming she's guilty of anything but caring for a man years before she met me.

"What?" She spins around so swiftly that the brush drops from my hand and onto the floor.

"I'll get that." I reach down knowing that I don't give a fuck about the brush. I need a minute to compose myself before I look into her eyes. I need to confront her about something that likely has no meaning anymore to her. I feel movement on the bed.

She's on her feet, pulling the robe tightly around her. I glance up to see her tucking the front of the robe together, covering the exposed skin of her chest. "Is this about my dad?"

Her dad? She hasn't spoke of him in months. I did wonder, briefly, why he wasn't at her sister's wedding but one thing I've learned about Jessica is that she won't share if she's not ready to. I've never pushed her about her relationship with her father. I won't.

"Your dad?" I parrot back, knowing that I should correct her immediately and ask about the senator. That's the right thing to do. It's what I want to do, but I sit on the edge of the bed, frozen.

"He wasn't at the wedding." She fidgets, moving back and forth from one foot to the other. It's something she's always done when she's emotionally uncomfortable.

"I noticed," I whisper. Why am I letting this conversation continue? It's become obvious, just from the time I've spent here with her family that none of them value their relationship with her dad. I don't think I heard anyone bring up his name once.

She pulls in a heavy breath before letting it seep slowly out between her lips. "My parents hate each other."

I want to leap to my feet and wrap her in my arms. She's shaking. "Jessica, let's not talk about them."

"He abandoned all of us." Her bottom lip quivers with the words. "It happened right before my sister graduated from high school. He left. One day he just moved without any real explanation."

My heart breaks at the words. I know his leaving impacted her deeply. I can see it now, within the expression on her face. "That must have been really hard for all of you," I say, quietly. I want to be supportive and loving. I want to be that compassionate guy who holds his girlfriend as she confesses about her past pain.

Her eyes scan my face as if she's looking for reinforcement behind my words. "Your parents are still together. It's hard for you to understand."

If anyone else spit those words at me, I'd take offence. I'd label them as jealous or envious, but I can't do that with Jessica. I was there when she met my parents and I saw the awestruck wonder in her eyes when they explained how they met more than thirty-five years ago. I watched her as she sat with my mother and looked at each and every picture in their wedding album. I know that she wishes her family would have traveled down the same path as mine. It kills me that it didn't work out that way for her. That's one of the reasons I want so desperately to marry her. I want to show her that she can have that life. I'll give her that life. Forever, with Jessica, is all that I want.

"I didn't mean that." She tosses me a weak apologetic glance. "I shouldn't have said that."

I stand in a single, fluid movement and pull her into my arms. "I know you didn't."

"It hurt that he wasn't there today, but…" her voice trails into the fabric of my shirt as she rests her face against my chest. "My sister didn't invite him. I don't think he even knew she was getting married today."

Each tender confession she's sharing is helping her feel closer. I can tell by the way she's clinging to me. The only problem is that with each word she speaks, I'm no closer to finding out about the senator.

Chapter 6

"Do you think I should invite my father to come see us for a visit?" Her hand drapes lazily over my thigh as I drive.

I stare down at it, knowing that if she has her way, I'll be barreling down the interstate with a raging hard-on in about thirty seconds. "Sure," I say absentmindedly.   After she confessed about her father not being invited to the wedding last night, she wanted to crawl into bed with me. I couldn't fuck her. After seeing the pain she was in, I knew that I couldn't take anything from her. I held her body next to mine until she fell asleep.

Her finger traces a faint path up my pant leg. "Are you going into the office when we get back?"

"I have to." I nod as I stare straight ahead at the congested roadway. "I'm dealing with a bitch of a case right now."

"The case is the bitch, or your client is the bitch?" She subtly tries to pull her hand free of mine. I know if I let it wander it's going to end up inside of my pants. I'd normally love that distraction, but not today. I need to get back to Manhattan and into the office.

I pull back on her hand, placing it in her own lap. "The client is a man. The case is a nightmare."

"Is there still something bothering you?" she asks in a hushed tone.

I glance back over my shoulder before changing lanes. I don't drive nearly enough. I pay a heavy ransom every month just to keep this car in a garage under my building. I miss being behind the wheel. When I lived in Boston, before moving to New York City, I drove almost everywhere. I still think about moving back sometimes, but with Jessica's career on the upswing, it's too much to ask. I refuse to bring it up again. I can live in Manhattan. Hell, I can live anywhere as long as Jessica is with me.

"Nathan?" She taps me lightly on the forearm. "What's bothering you? You've been quiet since we left Connecticut."

She's right. I have been quiet. I'm still reeling after hearing about the senator and now I've got to get my mind back into work mode. I'm grumpy and I'm frustrated with myself. I should have pushed through the unexpected discussion about her father last night and gotten to the bottom of what the senator meant to her. Christ, for all I know, Charity made up that bullshit so I'd take a ride with her in the backseat of her car.

"I need to talk to you about something." I take the weak willed way out and keep my eyes glued to the road. We're finally nearing the city, which means that the traffic is only getting worse.

"About work?" There's hope in the question.

"No." I look quickly to my side. My eyes dart over her face but I don't allow them to linger long enough to gauge her reaction. "It's something else." I don't want to sound so mysterious and foreboding. That's not who I am.

"Is it about us?" she presses. I can sense movement beside me. She's fidgeting. She's uncomfortable emotionally and her inner instinct to run is trying to take over.

I can't have this conversation while I'm weaving through mid-morning traffic. I won't have it. I reach blindly for her hand and feel an instant sense of relief when she laces her slim fingers through mine.

"You can tell me, Nathan."

"Jessica." I pull her hand to my lips "I love you. It's minor. We can talk about it tonight."

I feel her hand go limp. She's clearly not convinced that it's nothing. I'm not either. Tonight I'm going to ask her point blank about the senator so we can put this behind us.

***

"Mr. Moore, I don't think you fully grasp what I'm telling you."

I stare across my desk at the grey haired man who is leaning as far forward as he can without tilting onto the floor. "I understand completely, Mr. Wilkinson. You hired me to represent you and I'm doing just that."

"I was here last week." He taps his wrinkled hand on his forearm just above the worn, leathered band of his watch. "What have you done since then? It's been six days now."

I pull my hand across my brow. "I've been making phone calls on a daily basis, sir. I've had several meetings related to your case." Going into minute details right now is just a waste of my time and his. I'm getting paid a percentage of what he walks away from if I win his case. All this extra talking and meeting is cutting into my bottom line.

"How much do you think you're going to get me back?" His voice cracks.

I look up and see the worry that washes over his expression. Here's an almost eighty-year-old man who gave the majority of his savings to a high profile investment advisor who is now facing felony charges. He's looking at me as if I'm holding every answer to his financial future. In many ways, I am. Why the fuck did I even take on this case? Trying to juggle his concerns, with the opposing counsel's constant refusal to discuss a settlement is wearing on me.

"Mr. Wilkinson." I lean back in my office chair, hoping he'll follow suit. I'd feel so much better if he had more faith in me. He sought me out on the advice of the attorney who handled his late wife's estate. My friend, Garrett Ryan, steered Mr. Wilkinson in my direction with a warning. Garrett told me to get this right. He painted a picture of how broken Mr. Wilkinson had been after his wife's death a year ago. He was vulnerable and had fallen into the palm of an investment advisor who is now sitting in a small jail cell awaiting trial on a long list of security related charges.

"How much?" he spits the question back with a tap on the edge of my desk. "I need to know how much. My granddaughter and her kids are moving in with me next week. She left her bastard of a cheating husband. I've got a lot of mouths to feed."

Way to add another brick to the guilt load I'm already carrying on my shoulders, Mr. Wilkinson. "I'm doing my best." I am. I spend almost all my time awake thinking about this case.

"Do you have kids, Mr. Moore?"

I look up from my desk at his face. "I don't." I already know where this conversation is headed, and I'm considering diving under my desk to avoid the head on collision that is coming my way.

"My wife and I worked our entire lives to save money," he begins. "When she died, God rest her soul, I wanted to give more to my granddaughters."

I nod. He's told me this story several times since I took on his case, three weeks ago. Each time, since the first, I'm tempted to tell him that I've heard it. I suspect he knows he's repeating but he wants to share. It helps him. I can see it and hear it.

"I gave Anthony that money so he could make more money for me." He shakes his head as if he's warding off all thoughts of Anthony Mercado, the man he trusted his financial empire with. "He was kind, he was nice to me, he said he understood what I was feeling after Nancy died." His bottom lip trembles at the mention of his late wife's name.

I've heard enough stories about her to understand that she was a sweet loving and very devoted wife. The first time he spoke about her I thought about Jessica and what it would feel like if I lost her. I doubt like fucking hell that I would be able to make any rational decisions either. Anthony Mercado set his sights on Phil Wilkinson the month after his wife died. This guy wasn't an ambulance chaser. He was a fucking hearse chaser.

I take in a deep breath. "I can't imagine how hard it was to lose her." I must have said that same phrase to him a dozen or more times since I met him. Each time I say it holds more and more meaning.

"I feel like an idiot. I wanted to give my granddaughters a chance in life. They're both in broken marriages, they have children, and they need my help." He wrings his hands together. "Nancy and I were going to build a big house with the money from the investments. The girls and their kids were going to live with us. You have to get that back for me."

I push my hands against my desk, slowly pulling myself up. He's right. I have to do something. I can't let that asshole get away with this. "Leave it to me, Mr. Wilkinson. You picked the right man for the job." The words sound believable, now I just have to make them come true.

Chapter 7

"Did it go okay at the office today?" Jessica asks, as she picks at the vegetable ragout she made for the two of us for dinner.

I take a heavy mouthful of food and chew it slowly. I feel spent. After my meeting with Mr. Wilkinson, I had gone down to the bar down the street from my office. Two glasses of bourbon later and I still feel like shit. I know she's waiting to talk about what's bothering me." It was fine," I say before shoveling another forkful of food into my mouth.

She moves the food around on her plate. I've only seen her take a small bite. "I know you're under a lot of stress. I know your job isn't easy."

The words are meant to pacify me. She's not that interested in my job. It's not her fault. When we first got together she asked me a lot of questions about what I do for a living. Back then, I only was interested in one thing. I wanted to fuck and that was it. I hate that I didn't give her more of myself in the beginning. "It's just a tough case. There's a lot of pressure."

She picks up her glass of red wine and only takes a very small sip before she places it back down. "I know you can't talk about it. There's that whole lawyer and client confidentiality thing."

I nod. She's right. I can't give her the specifics. I can talk in generalities though. "My client lost everything. He lost his wife and his life savings almost at the same time."

She pulls her hand up to her chest as if she's warding off something that might touch her heart. "That's horrible, Nathan. Were they married a long time?"

I swallow what's left in my own wine glass. "They were married for fifty-four years."

She lets out a little gasp as if there's not enough air in the room." That's so long. They must have gotten married very young."

I don't want the words to bother me but they do. I'm thirty-two years old. I want to be married and I want to be a father. I want all of that with Jessica and I want it now. "He told me that he can't remember what it was like before he married her."

Her bottom lip trembles as if the words have cut right to her core. "That's beautiful. That's true love."

I push on, not to explain more about my client but to touch that part of her. I want her to be open and vulnerable. I want her to take inspiration from a love that is that deep and enduring. "The first day that I met him, he told me something."

She leans forward on the table, her elbows resting on either side of her plate. "What was it? What did he say?"

I mimic her stance and cover her hands with mine. I look straight into her beautiful blue eyes as I say, "he told me he was the luckiest. He said every day before he gets out of bed he thinks about her and how lucky he is to love her."

She looks down at our hands. "You mean how lucky he was to love her. I mean before she..."

"Died?" I interrupt. "No that's not what I mean."

She bites the corner of her bottom lip. I know that she's searching for the right thing to say. This conversation is touching her the same way it's touching me. "What do you mean?"

I swallow hard before I pull in a heavy deep breath. "He loves her as much today as he did the day he married her. He told me he'll never stop loving her. She owns the other half of his heart."

Her eyes fill with tears, her hands grab tightly to mine as she whispers the words, "You own my heart too. You do."

***

"What the hell you talking about?" I ask, the tone of my voice unmistakably loud and clear.

She pushes past me the entire time whispering something into the microphone attached to her earpiece. "I don't have time for this right now. Can't you see we're completely full?"

I quickly pull my eyes around the near capacity restaurant. "I don't care. Where the fuck is Jessica?"

She turns sharply to face me. "I'm a hostess. I'm not a babysitter. I don't know where Jessica Roth is. I do know that she called in sick only an hour before we opened. It's the third time in the past month."

The third time in a month? What the hell is going on? Jessica hasn't been sick. I stopped at the apartment on my way home from work to drop off my laptop and she wasn't there. I came here to see her because I felt badly about last night. I got called into conference call right after dinner. We were both overwrought with emotion after talking about Mr. Wilkinson and his wife's death.

"I don't have time to stand and talk to you." The hostess isn't very hospitable. "When you do see her you should tell her that she's on dangerous ground right now. There are a lot of people that want to work here."

I shift on my feet and step closer to her, blocking her path away from me. The only way around me is through me. "My name is Nathan Moore. I'm an attorney." Hell, yes, I'm going to play that card. "It sounds as though you're threatening Ms. Roth."

"You're an attorney," she says the words with obvious disdain. "I should've known by the suit. What's with all the suits who want to talk to Jessica? Is she in some kind of trouble?"

Again, I'm being thrown into the middle of the ring of confusion that is Jessica's life. "What did the other suit want?" Christ, let there be only one other man in a suit looking to talk to my suddenly popular girlfriend.

She scans her eyes over my face before they dart behind me. "I'm too busy for this. He looked like an attorney too."

I step forward a touch. Intimidating this woman isn't going to be easy. It's obvious that she thinks her hostess job is vital to the earth continuing to spin on its axis. "What did he look like?" I don't know why I'm asking. I have no idea what guy in a suit would be coming to talk to Jessica at work. I also have no clue why the fuck she hasn't talked to me about it.

She stomps her foot as if that's going to magically make me disappear. "He was older than you. I'd say he's even more handsome than you." There's no mistaking the spite dripping from that.

Whatever. Jesus, this woman is annoying as all fuck. She must be new, that, or she's so forgettable that I can't place her within my mind. "Did you see him talking to Jessica?" I know I sound desperate. That's because I am. Obviously, I need to look to anyone, including this stranger, to help me understand what's going on with the woman I'm sharing my bed with.

"Yes." Her eyes spring back to my face. "They talked in the corner and then she started crying and he took off." Her hand flies through the air past my head towards the entrance to Axel NY.

"He was only in here the one time?" The question doesn't come out with all the apprehension I'm feeling. Shit. Who is the guy she's talking about?

"No." She stops as if she's unwilling to share more. I'd venture a guess that it's more about her enjoying being the one in control. She knows she's dangling something I want right in front of my face and I'm going to have to acquiesce to whatever she wants to get it from her.

"Listen," I pause. My eyes search her plain black dress for a nametag. There's nothing.

"Sasha," she offers.

Sasha? Really? The only Sasha I knew was back in Boston. I met her in a club and she definitely lived up to the name. This Sasha looks like she doesn't even comprehend the meaning of the word sexy. She's serious, through and through.

"Sasha," I repeat back in as even a tone as I can muster. "Did the man who came to see Jessica only visit her here once?" That sounds semi-professional.

"You're dating her, aren't you?" She just went off the track at full speed. "I've seen you in here before. I saw your hand on her ass."

Guilty as charged. How am I supposed to keep my hands off Jessica? That's almost impossible. "We do date, yes." Stilted much, Nathan?

"Is she dating him too?" There's a question I never saw coming. "I mean, does she have a thing for lawyers?"

I pull my hands to my face, massaging my temples with brisk, easy circles. "She has a thing for me," I say with confidence. I'd bet my right hand and foot that Jessica's not cheating on me. That can't be what's going on. Maybe that's just my male pride talking, but the way that woman looks at me and the way she reacts to my body, I know there's little chance that she's jumping into another guy's bed.

"She kissed him."

The proclamation bounces around in my ears before it sinks into my brain. "Jessica kissed him?" I repeat back. I didn't hear that correctly. There's no way in hell Jessica put her lips on another man.

"I saw it with my own two eyes." Her hand darts into the air and she points at her face. "When she first saw him, she kissed him."

On the lips, I want to ask but I'm not a middle school kid who just found out his girlfriend made out with the opposing school's football team captain. I'm an accomplished lawyer, I own an apartment that borders on Central Park, I have more money than most people make in ten lifetimes. I'm confident. I don't fall to pieces because of a kiss.

"Sorry to break it to you." She taps me lightly on the shoulder.

"What?" I spit back.

"Sorry to be the one to tell you that Jess is getting it on with someone else." She breezes past me then and I don't try and stop her. I can't. I can't move. All I can think about is my beautiful Jessica, tucked into the arms of another man, her lips coursing hot over inch of him. My hand darts into the inner pocket of my suit jacket. I reach for the box. It's the same box I've carried with me for the past six months. It's my future. It's the ring I've been trying to give her. The same ring she'll never accept. Maybe now the reason is clear. It's not only clear; it's fucking wearing a suit.

Chapter 8

"Jessica," I scream her name as I charge through the door of our apartment. I went to the bar next to Axel after Sasha made me feel like a goddamn nothing. I had three bourbons and now I'm in prime argument mode. I've had to defend myself time and time again in this relationship. I've never cheated on Jessica. I've come clean with everything. Now it's her turn.

I'm greeted with sullen silence. I toss my suit jacket on the couch. My thumb traces a quick path over my smartphone's screen. I pull up my text messages. There isn't one response to the six text messages I've sent her in the past hour. Wherever the fuck she is right now, it's obvious I'm her last priority.

"Nathan?" Her voice enters the space before I even notice that she's opened the door. She couldn't have been more than a few feet behind me when I walked into the building. "Why are you standing in the dark?" She flips the light switch on and two cool, pale ceiling lights flicker on.

"I just got here." I don't turn to look at her. I swear I'll fucking lose it if she's standing there in her chef's jacket. If she lies to me about being at work I'll move out. I can't stomach the thought of another man kissing her. How the hell am I supposed to act if she's been fucking some other guy's brains out?

I hear her drop her purse on the table next to the door. The sharp rattle of her keys hitting the wood follows. "Did you work late?"

I don't want to be interrogated right now. "No." It's blunt and direct. It's a sign of how frustrated I am right now. "Did you?"

There's a heavy sense of hesitation in the air. I can hear her labored breathing. "No," she says quietly.

She doesn't expand and I have to grab the edge of the couch to steady myself. Christ, I love her so much. My heart is literally caving in right now. Don't let this be my reality. Please let there be some logical explanation for why she has been missing work. I need to hear that Sasha didn't actually see Jessica kissing anyone. I want a redo of this entire night.

"How was work?" I push the question out. I do it because I need a place to start. It's one of the fundamental principles I learned in law school. Give the defendant just enough rope to hang themselves.

I hear her shuffle her feet. I can't tell if she's pulling off her shoes or putting them back on so she can race back out the door. Jessica can't handle confrontation. If there's a fight, she's going to look for the nearest exit. I've worked hard with her, over the course of the past year, to push back on her natural instinct to race out of the room when we have an issue. Right now, I'm scared that if she runs, I may never see her again.

"Jessica," I say her name as much to gain her attention as to quiet my own raging confusion. "I asked you a question."

"I know." Her voice is low and edgy. I can hear the apprehension in it.

I flip around on my heel. It shouldn't be this complicated. I shouldn't have to ask her the same question twice before I get a definitive answer. It's a simple question. I just want an answer. "I…" my voice halts as I look at her. She's wearing one of my t-shirts under her black cardigan. The jeans she's wearing are rolled up at the hem but there's no mistaking that she stepped in a few puddles on her way home. Her hair is a matted mess. "Jessica." I reach for her but she takes a step back.

"You went to Axel." She nods as she says the words. "Sasha told me you were there."

She had a warning. She knew I'd be waiting for her with a mind filled with questions. "I was looking for you." I work hard to keep my voice even.

Her eyes scan my face. "I didn't feel well today."

"Are you sick?" That question is meant to be asked with compassion. It doesn't contain any of that when it leaves my lips. If it sounds as accusatory to her as it does to me, she's going to shut down.

She doesn't speak. Her head just drifts thoughtlessly from side-to-side.

I feel like I'm talking to my niece or nephew about a bad mark they got on a spelling test. There's no offer of assistance. She's not even trying to assuage my worry or concern. "What's going on?" I blurt the question out.

"Nathan." She takes a step towards me. "I'm sorry."

The words hit me with the same force as the first time she slapped me across my face when she thought I was cheating on my ex-girlfriend, Cassandra, with her. *I'm sorry.* The phrase is meant to placate and please. It's meant to chase away the bad deed and replace it all with feelings of hope and promise. All I can hear is the veiled confession of a woman who I love desperately. All I can see is her falling into the bed of a man who isn't me. All I know is that this is my future standing in front of me telling me that she's sorry.

"For what?" I know my voice is trembling. I can't control it. I don't want to hear her response but I know that I have to. This is the very reason why I avoided relationships most of my life. This is why I wouldn't allow my heart to feel too deeply.

"I've done things." Her breath hitches as she says the words. "I've been missing work."

I don't give a fuck about her work. I don't give a shit about anything other than the things that she's doing with the other guy who waltzed into Axel in a suit. The guy she kissed.

"Why?" I ask, trying desperately to not reach out and pull her into me. One part of me feels repulsed by the idea of her with anyone else. The other part of me is watching her tremble. She needs me to anchor her emotions. She needs to hold tight to me so she can find the strength within herself to confess. I fist my hands at my side, trying to ward off the almost compulsive need I feel to embrace her.

Her gaze drops to my hands and I see her tense. "I'm scared to tell you."

I've never harmed Jessica. I can't. It's not within the fabric of my body or soul to cause her any discomfort, other than the fleeting bite of it when I'm buried completely inside of her. "I won't hurt you, Jessica," I say the words to appease her. I need her to know that she's safe with me. Regardless of what she's about to confess, I'm not going to lash out. I can't either verbally or physically.

"I would never hurt you." Her tone is unyielding. "I would cut off my leg before I'd hurt you, Nathan."

I charge forward, pulling her small body into my chest. I rest my chin against the top of her head. I wrap my arms around her back. She's sobbing now. "Just tell me."

"I can't." Her hands skim across the front of my shirt. "I don't know how to."

I reach up to cup her cheeks in my hands. I graze my lips softly across her forehead. "You can tell me anything. I can tell you anything. This is us."

She nods as tears stream steadily from her eyes. "I love you more than anything, Nathan."

I see the promise of those words in her eyes. She means it. She's not just saying it to quiet something that is roaring within me. She's saying it because it's her truth. It's what she feels. I see it.

"Sasha said another man came to see you at Axel," I say the words gently. "Is it about him?"

Before I can react she pushes back, her face loses all of its color, her hands fly in the air and she's on her heel headed for the door.

"No, no, no…" she repeats over and over. "She had no right to tell you."

I don't move. I can't. Her reaction is screaming at me. "Don't walk out of here, Jessica."

She turns back, her face a cloudy mess of tears and anger. "You were checking up on me."

It's immature and thoughtless. She's retreating back to the same girl she was when I met her at the club. She's the girl who bolted at the first sign of trouble. "I was looking for you because I missed you." I don't mince the words. There's no reason to. It's the truth, plain and simple.

"You've been different since we got back from my sister's wedding."

I take a moment to process the statement. It's accusatory even if it's not meant to be. Is she seriously pushing this back on me? Is she going to blame me for what she's been doing? "What?" I bark the word out as I take a heavy step towards her. "Are you fucking kidding me, Jessica?"

She pushes her back into the door. Her hand leaps to the doorknob. It's instinctive. She's searching for her escape route if this gets too heavy. I have to admit, I'm impressed that she hasn't left the building in a mad dash yet. "No. I'm not fucking kidding you, Nathan," she hisses. "Something has been up your ass since then and you refuse to talk about it."

"You're right." My hand flies into the air and past her to settle on the door. I move forward again, trapping her where she's standing. "There is something up my ass."

"What?" She pulls her chin up in an act of defiance. She's not backing down. She's not going to retreat on this. "What the fuck happened there?"

I lean down, my lips hovering close to hers. I look her directly in the eyes as I very softly and clearly whisper. "The senator, Jessica. You fucked a senator."

Chapter 9

Time doesn't move for what feels like endless moments as her tear filled gaze jumps from my lips to my eyes. I watch as a veil of confusion overtakes her. Her knees buckle, her hands reach for the wood plank that is the door as she slowly slides down it.

"Jessica." I scoop my arm around her waist, catching her mid fall. "Jessica, please."

She doesn't speak. I don't know if it's because she's unwilling or if the weight of the air between us is holding her back. She raises her hand to shield her face. Her sobs overtake her. I hold her close, wishing I hadn't thrown that at her the way I did. She's fragile. She's always been too fragile for her own good.

"You should sit down." I scoop her up in my arms in one easy movement and carry her into the room. Her arms hang limp at her sides. Her eyes are staring a path straight through me. I place her down carefully on the couch.

"I'm sorry." The words escape her lips in such a quiet tone that I have to strain to make out each word. "I'm sorry," she repeats, this time no louder than the last.

I kneel in front of her. Any resistance that she was holding onto at the door has evaporated. She's broken and weak. She's rocking back and forth on the cushion, the rhythmic movement of her body making a sliding sound on the leather. It's the only sound invading the unending silence in the room.

"I'm sorry." The words are still so soft that I have to strain to hear them.

"Jessica." I place my hands on her knees. She doesn't pull back. "Jessica. I'm sorry too."

I expect her eyes to dart to mine for confirmation of the words but that doesn't happen. Instead, she pulls her head closer to her chest.

"Please look at me," I coax. I'm scared. I've pushed her into emotional places in the past but it's never been this way. She's never shut down so completely on me before. I regret bringing him up the way I did. I regret not asking about him right after the wedding, when she was so happy, open and composed.

"No," she says through a sob. "I can't."

I want to grab her shoulders and shake her. I want her to come back to me and talk about this. I want her to hold my face in her hands and tell me that she's overreacting and that all of it is just a simple misunderstanding. "I need you to listen to me, Jessica."

Her head darts up. I watch as her eyelids slowly open. She stares at my face, her eyes sweeping across my forehead, before settling on my mouth. "Please, Nathan." Her hand dashes from her leg to my arm. "Please."

"I'm not going anywhere." I reach forward to run my lips over her cheek. "I'm staying right here." I know I mean it right now. If she tells me she's been fucking the guy who was at Axel, I can't promise her anything.

She nods. Her hand moves up my arm. "Who told you?"

I pull her hand into my own and graze it across my lips. "I was talking to a woman at the wedding. Her name was Charity. She told me you were involved with a senator."

"Charity," she repeats the name as she stares past me to the wall. "Who is Charity?"

I can't say I'm surprised that she doesn't remember the woman. She was completely forgettable. "She looks like a librarian." I have no other point of reference so that's what pops out. "She said you went to school together."

Her brow furrows. "Does she have brown hair and glasses?"

"No glasses." I shake my head from side-to-side. "She has short brown hair."

The edge of her lip quivers slightly. "I think I remember her. What did she say to you?"

I decide that this moment calls for me to temper my unending need to tell Jessica everything. She doesn't want to hear about how Charity wanted to ride my dick in the back seat of her Cadillac. "She mentioned that you used to be involved with a man who was in the senate." It's a foreign statement, even now when I've had time to process the information. I'm not about to tell Jessica that after she went to sleep the first night we got back to New York that I spent hours online trying to decipher what senator Charity was talking about. I came up empty handed.

Her hand leaves my arm and jumps to her face. She rubs it across her eyes. "It was so long ago."

I feel instantly relieved. "Charity said it happened right after high school."

"That's when it started." It's a subtle correction but it's open ended. "I met him after high school."

I have so many questions floating from every corner of my mind at once. They're colliding. My senses are overwhelmed. "When did it end?"

"It was over before I met Josh."

I don't need the reminder of her ex-boyfriend. Hell, I don't want to talk about any of this. I want her to go back to being the Jessica Roth I seduced at the club that night I first laid eyes on her. I was the one who seduced her, right? She wasn't preying on me, was she?

"When's the last time you saw him?" It's a selfish question. I'm not asking because I want to give her an opportunity to cleanse her soul. I'm asking because I want to know when the last time the fucking senator drove his cock into my beautiful Jessica's tender body.

"Today."

Chapter 10

I recoil on my heels. My hands leap from her body at the same time. Fuck. She just fucking said she saw the goddamned senator today.

"Nathan?" Nothing follows my name. What the fuck kind of question is that?

"What?" I'm on my feet now. I can't breathe. I blindly reach for my tie, pulling on the knot. I throw it beside her on the couch once I get it free. I still can't get enough air in my lungs. I rip open the first two buttons of the white dress shirt I'm wearing. They tumble silently to the hardwood floor.

"I didn't do anything." It's weak. It's so goddamned weak that I don't fucking believe it.

I turn so my back is to her. I can't look at her right now. My anger is right there. It's right at the surface and if I don't temper it, I'm going to say things that I'll never be able to take back. They're the things she said to me back when she discovered a cell phone I had filled with the names of hundreds of women I'd fucked. How the hell did she get over that? I can't even think straight right now. "What the fuck does that mean?"

"I didn't sleep with him…" The pause does little to control my ever growing rage. "Not today, I didn't sleep with him today."

"Today?" I hurl the word at her as I turn back around. My hands are on my cufflinks now, pulling thoughtlessly at them. I'm overheating. The room suddenly feels like it's the middle of summer and I'm standing in my suit on a crowded street. "You didn't fuck the senator today?"

"Thomas," she counters. "I didn't fuck Thomas today."

Thomas. He has a fucking name. Of course he does. She didn't let that detail escape without reason. Why the hell is she making this more personal? I don't want to know his name. I don't want to know anything about him.

"He was at the wedding." She nods as if she's reminding herself of the fact. "He was at Julie's wedding."

I roll up the arms of my shirt. The act not just meant to help me cool down physically, but emotionally as well. I was so focused on keeping her away from Josh Redmond, that piece of shit ex-boyfriend of hers, that I didn't even notice that another man she fucked was in the room. "Did you talk to him?"

She nods quickly. "I did. It was only for a minute."

"Where the fuck was I?" I ask, knowing that it sounds territorial. It's who I am though. I'm not going to hide behind a veil of something I'm not to appease her right now. I can't believe she talked to him that night and today. All of this is spurring on my own desire to bolt.

"I don't know," she tosses the words back effortlessly. "You were talking to a lot of different people that night."

Women. It's what she wants to say. I was talking to a lot of women. The majority of them were related to Jessica in some way. I spent a good portion of that night trying to dodge her mother's overly zealous hands. I also spent more than an hour listening to her grandmother and aunt tell me stories about Jessica as a little girl. Who knew that while I was tripping down memory lane with her relatives that she was reacquainting herself with an ex-lover?

"I was getting to know your family," I hiss the words out slowly. "I was trying to become part of your family." My index finger darts in her direction.

I can't tell if the words register or not. She's stoic. "It meant nothing, Nathan."

"What meant nothing?" I take a heavy step towards her as the words leave me. "Talking to him that night meant nothing? Or talking to him today?"

"He's a part of my past." It's a diversion. She's avoiding the question.

I push my hand through my hair in exasperation. "At that fucking door…" My hand juts to the right towards the apartment door. "At that door when I brought him up you practically fainted. What the fuck was that about?"

"I came home to tell you." She pulls her gaze down to the floor. "I wanted to tell you since the wedding."

"Why didn't you?"

"I knew you'd react," she begins before looking directly at me. "I knew you'd react like this."

She's right. How am I supposed to argue a point that is so blatantly correct? I always flip out over Jessica and other men. My blood boils whenever I see a guy checking her out on the street. I almost physically lose it if I hear anyone trying to pick her up. It's no fucking surprise that she'd try to shield both of us from that.

"You always pitch a fit about me and other men." She shrugs her shoulders. "Thomas and I haven't seen each other in years. I was surprised at the wedding. I didn't want to ruin our night."

Our night? That was the night she wanted to fuck me senseless in the elevator. It was the night she took my cock in her mouth the minute we were back in our hotel room. She couldn't keep her greedy hands off of me. "Did you blow me that night because you were thinking about him?" I regret the words the instant they leave my lips. They're meant to hurt her. Their intention isn't shrouded in anything. They're hot, piercing and they make a direct hit.

Her mouth falls open. She slowly stands. She reaches to the arm of the couch for balance. I wait for her to walk towards me, half expecting her to scream a litany of curse words at me. She stops right in front of me.

"Christ, Jessica." I reach towards her. "I didn't mean that. I fucking didn't mean any of that."

She takes a small step back, so she's just out of my reach. Her hand juts into the air between us. "I have nowhere else to go." Tears stream down her face now. "I'm going to sleep in the guest room."

"No." I move to grab her elbow to stall her. I can't let her walk out of this room. I don't want her to think constantly about my spiteful, petty words as she tries to drift off to sleep. "Listen to me, Jessica."

She rips her arm from my grasp. "There's nothing left to say, Nathan. Nothing."

I don't try and stop her. I only stand with my regret as she walks down the hallway.

Chapter 11

"Thomas Lane is your girlfriend's ex? Governor Lane?" Garrett can't hide his amusement at the statement. "When the fuck did that happen? Didn't she just graduate from high school?"

Jessica's age has always been fodder for Garrett's incessant joking about her. I've known him since law school. I know him well enough to realize that he's incapable of being serious when it comes to her. That's because he's so fucking jealous that I'm with her and he's still alone.

"Shut the hell up," I bark across my desk at him. "You know she's not that young. It happened when he was still a senator."

"How did you find out?" His tone shifts. It's actually more serious which is saying a lot for him. "When did you find out?"

"Last night." I pinch my index finger and thumb across my nose. "I railed on her about skipping work when she got home and somehow we ended up talking about that shit head."

"Shit head?" He cocks a brow. "Governor Lane is responsible for a lot of the positive change in Connecticut."

He sounds like a goddamned campaign commercial. I won't be surprised if he puts a pin on my lapel with the Governor's face on it. I can't stand his face. After Jessica went into hiding in the guest room, I did another search for senators in Connecticut named Thomas. It took all of a split second before his smiling face was staring right back at me. As much as I hate to admit it, Sasha was right; the Governor is easy on the eyes. I could instantly see why Jessica would have fallen for him.

"I don't care about him." It sounds petulant and juvenile. "I care about Jessica."

"So she used to bang him back in the day." He leans back in the chair. "You're no angel, Nate."

I don't need the reminder. I've been playing that argument in my mind since Jessica walked out of the room. I don't have a right to be angry. I can't even remember the majority of women I've fucked. Why the hell am I letting this get so far under my skin? She fucked some guy years ago and now he's back sniffing around her. Who can blame him? "I know," I acquiesce.

"Why do you even care?" He crosses his right leg over the left. "It happened a long time ago, right?"

I nod. I'm hoping it was a long time ago. The only grain of faith Jessica threw my way last night was that she hadn't fucked him yesterday. My logical mind is telling me that he hasn't been inside of her in years. My childish, jealous and petty mind is telling me that he's on the chase right now, trying to get that sweet, tight, little body of hers back in his bed. "It was years ago."

"That makes sense. I mean he's married now."

My head bolts up. Why didn't I read the articles last night instead of just staring at the guy's picture? "He's married?"

Garrett cocks a brow. "How do you not know any of this?"

"How long has he been married?" Maybe his interest in Jessica is nothing more than a quick jaunt down memory lane. Maybe he's in New York on something unrelated to her and he tracked her down at Axel.

"I don't know." He shrugs his shoulders. "He and his wife have a couple of kids."

That information only adds to my relief. There's no way in hell Jessica would get herself wrapped up in a relationship with a married man. I feel like shit. I feel like an ass for getting on her case about some guy she banged when she was a teenager. "I need to get some flowers." I reach for the phone on my desk.

"By the sounds of it…" Garrett dips his chin in the direction of the phone. "You should probably order every bouquet they have."

***

"I liked the flowers." Her head doesn't move as the words leave her lips. She hasn't glanced in my direction since I sat down next to her on this bench in Central Park. "I left them at the restaurant. I'll pick them up on my way home."

"I stopped by there to see you." I inch closer. "I didn't know you were on the early shift today." It's true. I had no idea what shift she was working. When I knocked softly on the guest room door early this morning there was no answer. I didn't press. I wasn't going to push her into a place where she would completely shut down on me.

She nods, her gaze still cast forward. "I just needed some time to cool down."

It's more than she would have given me a few months ago. I take it. I fucking embrace it. "I was out of line, Jessica."

"You were an asshole." The corner of her mouth snaps up in a small grin. She offers me the soft baked pretzel she's holding in her hand.

I pull off a piece before popping it into my mouth. I knew she'd be here the moment the head chef at the restaurant told me her shift was done. It's the place she always comes to when she needs to think. "You're right." I pull off another piece. "I'm fucking starving."

"You always say that." Her head turns towards me. "You eat a lot."

"Lucky for me you're an amazing chef." My tone is light and cheerful. I'm not trying to mask the depth of what happened last night. I'm trying to find a spot where she'll let me back in. I want her to know that I didn't fucking mean what I said.

She reaches up to scratch her fingers along the side of her face. "I wish you would have been my first."

The words tear through me with more strength than I can bear. My heart jumps in my chest. I have to pull my finger across my brow to temper the heavy onslaught of emotions I'm feeling. "Jessica."

"You don't have to say you wish I was your first." She bites her bottom lip. "I'm not looking for that."

I know she's not. I also know that she's well aware that if I could change anything about my past, before I met her, I would. I was aimlessly searching for something within all those women. Every encounter I had was more vacant and empty than the one before it. I was on autopilot, fucking a new woman almost every week, just to satiate the empty pit that was inside of me. It only grew larger until Jessica walked into the club.

"I know, Jessica," I say the words to quiet my own emotions. I know she accepts me exactly as I am. She's overlooked so much bullshit for me. Why the fuck am I making such a huge deal over a man she slept with so long ago?

"Sasha told me she talked to you about him." She hands me the remaining piece of pretzel. "She told you that I kissed Thomas."

I nod. "She did."

"That's not what happened." She sighs heavily. "He kissed me when I walked out of the kitchen. I thought you were there to see me."

"Me?"

"Sasha came to the back and said that a gorgeous man in a suit wanted to talk to me." Her hand taps my leg. "You're the only gorgeous man in a suit I want to talk to."

I feel sudden elation at the words. I don't need confirmation that Jessica loves me. I see it every day when I wake up next to her. I feel it in her kiss and in the way she holds my hand. "I like being that guy. I want to always be that guy."

"I made so many mistakes, Nathan." Her hand reaches for mine. "I wish I could redo parts of my life."

I hold her hand tightly in mine as people rush past us, oblivious of the weight of the conversation we're having. "I have that same wish, Jessica. I think most people do."

"Maybe." She glances at me. "It's different for me."

"Why?" I squeeze her hand, encouraging her to let it out. I want her to confess. I want her to crack open and let everything out that she's been holding tightly to.

"I was so young." She shakes her head. "I thought I knew everything about love back then."

Love. It's the first time that word has popped up when she's been talking about Thomas. "Did you love him?"

Her gaze catches mine for a brief moment. I see the confusion in her brow. She pushes her hair back from her face before she responds, "Who?"

I take more comfort in her response than I should. I'm certain that she's just confused if I'm talking about Thomas or Josh. Right now, I don't give a shit. I want the only man who has ever owned her heart to be me. I'm greedy like that. I want that to be our reality even if it's completely unrealistic. "Thomas," I answer because I have to. I can't stall this conversation because of my own insecurities.

"Can you love someone before you know yourself?"

I don't know the answer. "I didn't love myself before I met you." That's my truth. I was never in love with anyone until Jessica pulled me out of my selfish shell and showed me what love was.

"I don't know if I even love myself now." Her shoulders surge forward a touch with the words. "Maybe I've never loved myself."

"You're an amazing person." I inch closer to her on the bench before I pull my arm around her shoulders. "You're the best person I know."

"I'm not." She shakes her head so swiftly from side-to-side that her hair bats against my shoulder. "I'm not a good person, Nathan."

I squeeze her body into mine, trying to will away all her self-doubts. I've seen this side of her before. She's long blamed herself for Josh's grandfather's death. Jessica was alone with him when he suffered a massive heart attack. She believed the medical training she had as a paramedic should have been enough to bring him back from the edge of death. The truth was that no one could have saved the man's life. The problem was that Josh drilled his version of reality into her brain for months after. She still blames herself for that death. I see the same self-loathing seeping out of her now.

"You're going to tell me I'm wrong." Her hand juts out into the air as if to stop me from speaking. "This time I'm right though. I've done things that good people wouldn't do."

I want to believe her words but I know from experience that she always views things from the edge of drama. She's likely making a mountain out of what I would consider a lowly molehill. I'm not going to insult her by telling her she's exaggerating. "We all make mistakes, Jessica."

She moves slightly so she can face me directly on the bench. "My mistakes aren't like your mistakes."

"I can't compare," I offer. "You haven't told me about yours."

She recoils slightly as if the words burn through her. She holds her composure though. "What if you leave me?"

"Have you fucked him since you've been with me?" I need to ask. It's a question that's been hanging on the edge of my tongue since I found out he was back in her life.

She doesn't answer immediately. Her fingers tap on mine. "What do you think, Nathan?"

Her constant refusal to answer a question with a question is alluring at times. It's fun and speaks of her need to protect her heart. Right now, in this instant, it's doing nothing but fueling my overactive imagination. "No questions, Jessica. Just tell me. Have you fucked him since you've been with me?"

"No." There's absolutely no hesitation in the word. It's calm, it's controlled and it's heard loud and clear.

Chapter 12

"He was married."

The words come from the doorway of my office. My head bolts up. She's standing there wearing the same dress she was months ago when she came to break up with me. Now, she's confessing one of her darkest sins to me.

"Did you hear me?" She takes a step into the space before she slams the door behind her. "I said he was married."

"I heard you." I don't get up. I did the math in my head last night after we got home from the park. I read everything I could get my hands on about the Governor. I knew that the son-of-a-bitch seduced my girlfriend, when she was an innocent teenager, into his bed.

She sits in one of the chairs, her entire body shaking. "I told you my mistakes were worse than your mistakes."

I stand now. I can't allow her to beat herself up over something that happened so long ago. "Jessica," I whisper her name as my lips graze over her forehead. I lean back against the edge of my desk as I look down at her. "I'm reasonably sure that at least a few of the women I fucked were married."

She closes her eyes and shakes her head as if she's warding off the mental image of me sliding my cock into someone else's wife. "Don't say that."

"It's true." I lean forward. "You were too young to know better. It's all on him."

Her fingers dart to her eyes. She pushes on her brows. "You don't know that."

"I know his type." I kneel down in front of her. "You were available and naïve. He took what he could from you."

Her body shifts when she pulls in a heavy breath. "It's not like that."

I know enough about women to know that there isn't one alive who is willing to confess that she was seduced by an older man just for sex. They all want to believe that love was woven into the fabric of the relationship somewhere. Maybe that's a coping mechanism. Maybe they have to tell themselves that so they can get over the fuckers once they're dumped.

"He didn't seduce me, Nathan." I hear the denial in her tone. She needs to believe that. It's very hard to picture a teenager Jessica not being on the receiving end of a lot of male attention.

I don't want to press this, but it's pushing a wedge between us. We haven't fucked since we got back from the wedding. She's been avoiding me and it's killing me inside. "He did."

She taps her hand on the arm of the chair. "You're wrong. You don't know."

I hear the edge of anger in her tone. She's trying to control herself. "I know his type," I hiss the words out. If she's going to fight me on this, I'm going to fight back. We're clearing the subject of Thomas the Governor off our collective intimate plate right now. I'm not going to let that bastard interfere in my relationship with Jessica another minute.

"I seduced him." She tips her chin out. "I made him want me and then I'm the one who fucked him."

I stand and lean back on my desk. My fingers curl over the edge of it, as much for steady balance as to curb my desire to clear everything off of my desk in one fell swoop. There's no hiding my anger at this moment. I just listened to the woman I love confess to seducing a married man. Sweet and innocent Jessica Roth just left the building. No wait. She just fell off the fucking planet.

"You don't know what I was like when I was eighteen."

I don't. She's right. I only know what she's like the past year and a half. I know that the woman I met at the club was anxious and nervous about having a one night stand with me. I know that she used her body in ways that surprised me given the limited experience she claimed to have. I know that she can suck cock better than anyone who has wrapped their lips around me. Maybe I don't know her as well as I think. "Did you know he was married?"

She pushes herself back into the office chair as if that's going to help her gain some distance from the question. "That's not important."

There's my answer. It just slapped me across the side of my face. "You knew."

She shakes her head slightly. "I knew he was involved with someone. It was right around the time they got married."

It's enough to placate me. I don't fucking care if he was married. That's on him. He should have kept his dick inside his pants if he was planning a walk down the aisle. "When did it end?" Again, it's a question that has no bearing in the here and now. Why the fuck does it matter when it ended? Why can't I just accept that the woman I'm hell bent on marrying has more of a sordid past than I realized?

"Months after it started." She shuffles her heels against the carpeted floor.

"Who ended it?"

"Why does that matter?" Her head tilts to the side. "It's over now. It's been over for years."

I know she's right. It doesn't matter. It shouldn't but I need to know. "Who ended it, Jessica?" I repeat the question as if I've heard nothing she's said in response to the first time I asked it.

She skims her hands over the skirt of her dress. "It was mutual. We both ended it."

That's not what I wanted to hear. The jealous part of my heart wanted her to say that she dumped him because she realized he was all wrong for her. I want her to tell me that she knew she'd find someone better and then I came along.

"I didn't know he'd be at the wedding, Nathan." Her hand brushes over the leg of my pants. "I wouldn't have gone if I knew he was there."

"Is that why you were so reluctant to agree to it?" The question first occurred to me when she told me that Thomas had been at the wedding. All the pieces of the puzzle had finally fit together. It made sense that she'd try to avoid going to a celebration where she knew he'd be.

"No." Her hand drops from me back into her own lap.

"You should have told me that night, Jessica." I try not to sound as annoyed as I am. "You should have told me you saw him."

"You see women all the time that you fucked."

I hate when she pushes my past back at me. I cringe when she uses it as a tool to hide behind her own flaws. "I saw one once." It had only happened once. For a split second in time, a woman I fucked back in Boston was working as a waitress at Axel NY. Her name is Alexa. She couldn't even register our night together in her mind. Jessica and I had laughed about it together later that night.

"You only told me about the one, Nathan." She holds up her index finger to exaggerate her point.

I cross my arms over my chest. Her need to divert during every important conversation is exasperating. I'm not going to pay forever for the sins she thinks I committed before we met. "Jessica. Why is he in New York?"

"He's here for me." She doesn't even attempt to sugar coat it. "He came here to talk to me."

"I want to meet him." I step back behind my desk and reach for the phone on my desk. "Do you still have his number? Give it to me."

"I don't have it," she says it too effortlessly for it to be a lie. She always hesitates before she says anything that isn't one hundred percent the truth. "He tried calling me I think but I didn't answer it."

"You don't have his number?" I ask. I don't even try and hide the surprise in the question. I assumed, because of my overly active jealous imagination, that they had been in constant contact since the weeding.

"No." She reaches down and pulls her small tan purse into her lap. I watch in silence as she shifts through it. "You can check my phone and see for yourself."

It's a gesture born out of her need for transparency in our relationship. After she'd stumbled on a phone I kept filled with women's numbers, I've left me phone within her arm's reach whenever we're in the same place. We have an unspoken understanding that she can pick it up and scroll through it whenever she wants. I have nothing to hide.

"Take it and see." She pushes it towards me.

I don't give in to the overwhelming temptation I feel to rummage through it at warp speed. I need to show her that I believe in her as much as she believes in me. "I don't need to." I want to. I fucking want to rip that phone out of her hand and search every single text message, email and call.

"You don't need to talk to him." It's a statement that's ripe with unspoken innuendo. "I told him not to contact me anymore."

"When did you tell him that?" I cock a brow.

"Yesterday."

I want to probe her about why she didn't mention it to me before now, but I bite my tongue. "Did he leave New York?"

Her gaze falls down to her hand. I watch as she taps her index finger and thumb together. "I don't know. I told him to stay away from me."

"Jessica." I kneel down now, my left knee touching the floor. "When you don't share things with me, my mind jumps to places it shouldn't be going."

She nods in understanding. Her hand glides over my cheek. "I know, Nathan."

"If you would have told me at the wedding about him, we could have cleared it up that night." It's wishful thinking on my part. She didn't bring him up because she wasn't ready to. That's what I'm telling myself. It may have much more to do with the fact that she wanted to talk to him before she shared any of it with me. I want to believe that she's as much an open book as I am, but these past couple of weeks aren't doing anything to bolster that.

"I love you so much." Her thumb pad skims over my lips. "I knew you'd blow your lid."

I smile at the words. She's right. I've proven that to her. The past few days I've been on edge just holding within me the knowledge that she was talking to a man she once shared a bed with. "That's why you should have told me right away," I press. "I could have blown my lid back in Connecticut. I would have helped you when he showed up here."

"I didn't need help." She stares at my lips. "I needed to handle it myself."

I nod in understanding. I want to press her about why she skipped work and what was so important that he had to travel all the way from Connecticut to see her. The questions are all sitting there, in queue, waiting for me to ask them. I can't right now. All I can do is accept what she's told me. Pushing her more now won't get me any closer to what I want. I want this woman to be my wife and if that means accepting that she has a few skeletons in her closet, I'll do it. I have to. I can't live without her.

Chapter 13

"Mr. Moore, unless you get me some results soon, I'm going to have to find another attorney."

Threats aren't my thing. Correction. They are my thing if I'm threatening Jessica with the promise of a mind blowing orgasm. Technically, you might argue that it's not a threat at all. I know, for certain, she'd argue that it's not a threat. I need to make her come. I'm going to stop by the restaurant tonight to whisper sweet nothings all about fucking in her ear.

"Are you even listening to me, Mr. Moore?" His voice breaks through my fantasy of licking Jessica's beautiful, round tits.

"Mr. Wilkinson." I try to focus on his face. It's jarring after the gorgeous images that were just dancing in my head.

He taps his cane against the carpeted floor and it does little for effect. The sound is muffled. "I can find someone else to help me if you aren't willing."

He can't. He may think he can but the contract I had him sign is air tight. He's not going anywhere whether he realizes it or not. "There's no need for that," I offer in a half ass genuine tone. The man had been chasing me down almost every hour upon the hour for the last two days. I've had my secretary soak up much of his ill placed attitude. He's frustrated with the limited progress I've been making on his case. I can't blame him. It's slow going but I'm getting somewhere and with a little patience, he may just see at least some of his money back in his hands within the next year or two.

"I'll have more to report at the end of the week." I stand, indicating that the meeting is now adjourned.

Mr. Wilkinson doesn't move at all. "We're not done."

"We're done." I nod. "The more time we spend chatting, sir, the less time I have to work on your case." I just pulled that out of thin air. I'm impressed.

"Good point." He teeters helplessly in the air for a brief moment as he pulls himself to his feet.

I walk around my desk to offer a hand but he swats it away. I don't take offense. The man is proud. I've sensed that the first moment he walked into my office. "I'll call you on Thursday," I say as I open the door and watch him walk through.

"You're Moore?" An unfamiliar voice from the left pulls my gaze away from Mr. Wilkinson at the bank of elevators.

I tilt my head to the left. My hands immediately jump into the pockets of my pants. If I let them roam free one of them is going to connect with his face. It's him. Governor Thomas Lane is standing less than two feet away from me.

***

"I thought you left town." I don't motion for him to sit. I don't care if he stands. I just want the bastard out of my office and my girlfriend's life as soon as possible.

"Jessie told you that?" The name is remote and ill-suited to her. I've never viewed her as anyone but Jessica. Jessie is the person she was back in Connecticut. I've heard countless other people call her Jess or Jessie. I've always struggled to connect with that.

"Jessica told me she asked you to leave her alone," I say in an even tone. "Why the fuck are you still here?"

He chuckles. I stare at him as he finally lowers himself into the chair Mr. Wilkinson was just sitting in. I can see why Jessica was drawn to him. It's obvious he's attractive. He's older than me. I'd guess by more than a decade. His brown hair is showing the first touches of grey. His blue eyes are honed in on me. "You're an attorney."

It's a statement, not a question. He's either heard about me from Jessica or the man has done his research. "That's not news, Governor."

He tips his head in my direction. "Jessica told me about you."

I feel a rush of pride at the comment. She didn't try and hide the fact that she was involved with someone. "Why are you here?"

He leans forward in his chair. His voice takes on a whispered tone. "Did she explain the confidentiality agreement to you?"

I try in vain to temper my reaction to his words. He didn't just say that there's a confidentiality agreement in place? I scratch my finger behind my ear trying desperately to find something to say in response that isn't going to make me look like he just threw a sucker punch at me and hit me square between the eyes. "We don't have secrets."

"You do." He rests his elbow on the arm of the chair. His simple gold wedding band catches the overhead light as he shifts his hand. "If you don't, Jessie is in a lot of trouble."

I hate every single word that just came out of his vile mouth. I hate that his mouth has kissed her and touched her in places I have. "Is this why you came to New York?" My hand flies behind me to the bank of windows that overlook mid-town Manhattan. "You came here to intimidate Jessica?"

"I came here to remind her that she needs to keep her pretty little mouth shut." He snaps his fingers together with a loud pop. "She brought up something at the wedding that she's not permitted to talk about. I came here to remind her of the consequences if she shares that information with anyone."

There's no way in hell he's talking about their affair. I need clarification about what's going on. "Jessica signed an agreement?"

"She signed an agreement," he begins as he taps his index finger on the edge of my desk. "She also took a huge check for her …" his voice trails. A thin smile takes over his lips. "She took money in exchange for her silence. There's a small matter regarding our affair that she can never talk about."

I stare at his smug face. He's got me by the balls and he knows it. He didn't waltz in here to ask me if Jessica broke the confidentiality agreement that he made her sign. He came here specifically to throw their past relationship in my face. "You can leave." I motion towards the door of my office.

"You're a lucky man, Moore." He slowly pulls himself from the chair.

I don't respond. I don't move an inch. I refuse to give him the satisfaction.

"I've yet to meet a woman who knew how to blow me the way she did." The words are clear, cold and meant to rile me.

I rush to my feet. My hands knot into fists at my sides. "Get the fuck out," I hiss through clenched teeth.

He raises a hand. "When you see her, tell her I miss her."

"Shut the hell up you bastard," I call after him as he opens the door and steps through it without looking back.

Chapter 14

"Jessica," I call her name before I've even got the door to the apartment open. "Jessica."

I step through into the entryway and realize immediately that she's already here. Her black flats rest near the doorway, her coat is tossed recklessly over the back of the couch and her purse is sitting on the small table next to the door.

My intention was to come home immediately after that fucking asshole, Thomas, left my office. I wanted to come here and decompress before I went to the restaurant. In my mind, I saw myself confronting her there, at work. It was a plan with no merit. Thankfully, I was called into a meeting about the Wilkinson case. I've spent the past three hours listening to numbers being tossed around, along with terms. I'm getting close to a settlement. I should be happy but the only thought that has been running through my mind is what Jessica agreed to be quiet about. What the fuck happened between her and the Governor?

I slide my suit jacket off before I call her name once more. I'm greeted with nothing but dead silence. She's somewhere in this apartment ignoring me. I bet that asshole called her after leaving my office to give her a heads-up. She knows I know about their agreement. She's going to be ready, with emotional guns blazing, to counter everything I say.

I head down the hallway, stopping first at the master bedroom. The bed is made. She pulled the linens back into place this morning after we'd gotten up. I wanted to fuck her the moment she opened her eyes, but she had lazily rolled out of the bed to make coffee. I didn't want to believe that she was avoiding sex on purpose, but it was feeling more and more like that every day.

I turn on my heel and dart my eyes into my office. She's not there either. It doubles as a guest room and that bed looks untouched too. I stand in place, listening intently. I hear the faint sound of water running. I bolt down the hallway towards the guest bathroom. I swing open the door to a haze of steam.

"Jessica," I say her name blindly into the space. "Jessica, I'm here."

The only response is the veiled sound of sobbing. She's crying. I can hear her labored breaths. Christ, what the fuck has got her so torn up? What is Thomas holding over her head?

I step closer to the marble shower stall. I look down to where her chef's jacket and black pants are tossed on the floor. Her bra and panties are settled on the floor nearby.   "Jessica," I whisper her name into the space. I don't want to alarm her. I don't want to scare her back into herself. She's vulnerable right now. She's open and raw. I need to get her to trust me. I want an explanation for what's going on with her and that fucking Governor.

"I'm home," I call into the stall. I can see the outline of her body through the fogged glass of the door. "Jessica, I'm here."

The sobbing stops abruptly. "I'm just having a shower." Her voice is muted. I can tell she's covering her mouth with her hand, trying to curb her emotions.

I swing open the door. She's not facing me. Her hands are gathered over her face. She's pressing her body into the damp wall, the water beating a path down her bare back.

"Jessica," I reach through the spray to touch her skin, not caring that the arm of my shirt is now drenched. "Please, Jessica, tell me what's going on."

She recoils when my fingers brush over her skin. She steps to the side knowing that she's out of my reach. "I just need a few more minutes." The words are soft and steady.

"No." I step into the shower, the water barreling down on me, soaking all my clothes instantly. My hands are on her back, pulling her into my chest. "You're falling apart inside, Jessica. Let me help you."

Any resistance she may have felt washes down the drain with the water. She falls into my body, her hands grasping tightly to mine as they circle her waist.

"Tell me, Jessica," I whisper into her ear. "Tell me what's happening."

She turns instantly and her hands are on my shirt. She's pulling at the buttons, trying desperately to rid me of my clothes. I try to catch her hands. I need her to stop. I can't want her right now. My cock can't respond the way it is. I'm hard just from staring at her nude, wet body.

"Don't." I grip tightly to her wrists. "Don't make this about sex."

Her eyes catch mine with a heated gaze. "You want me," she whispers against my lips. "You want me, Nathan."

I do. I can't deny that. It would be an obvious lie. My cock is straining against my pants. I want to push her against the shower wall, pull her thighs around my waist and drill my cock into her until she's screaming my name. I want that more than anything in this moment.

Her lips are on mine before I have time to think. She slides her tongue over my bottom lip, forcing its way into my mouth. I grip her hair, tilting her head so I can claim more of her with the kiss. She melts into my touch.

"Please, fuck me, Nathan." The words fall from her lips into mine. "I need to feel you inside of me."

My better judgement falls to the wayside as I pull my soaked clothes from me. I'm on my knees in front of her, drawing her smooth legs apart. I hoist the left one over my shoulder. I don't waste a moment before I graze my tongue over her moist folds.

She juts her hips out as her back presses into the shower wall. The warm water continues beating down on us both. I can't stop myself. I've been craving the taste of her for days. I need to give her this. I have to show her that I want her. I need her to feel that we're still connected on this very basic level.

"Yes," she whispers into the heated space.

I take my time, carefully twirling my tongue over her clit. I know that she likes it slow and steady. She loves when I build up the tension by drawing the orgasm slowly out of her. I pull my tongue down, darting into her entrance, scooping up the sweet desire that is already flowing out of her. She's wet. Even though we're in the shower, and the water is coursing over us both, I can tell that she's so wanting. She needs to come. I need to give that to her.

"Please, like that." The words fall from her lips as her hands twist in my wet hair. She pulls sharply in an effort to guide my tongue back to her clit.

I give her everything she wants. I lick my index finger slowly before pushing it into her slick channel. I stroke it in and out at an even pace as I twist her swollen bud around my tongue. I lick her harder and faster. Her sex clenches around my finger so I slide another in. She's so tight. Her body is involuntarily responsive to mine.

Her hips buck slightly as she nears her release. "Nathan, please." Her voice gets lost in the beat of the water on my back.

I pull her clit between my teeth while I pound my fingers in and out of her pussy. I sense her body tense. I feel the wetness around my hand as she throws her head back and a deep moan escapes from her as the orgasm washes slowly through her body.

I don't move. I keep licking, probing and sucking. I need another. I want to hear her call my name again. She's giving me as much in this moment as I'm giving her. I feel close to her. We're connected in this small space in the most primal way.

I hear her head hit the shower wall again as her entire body convulses in a long, slow orgasm. I hold tight to her waist, letting her come down from the edge with my lips still against her. I finally feel her leg go limp on my shoulder. I carefully pull it down.

"Fuck me, Nathan." It's a statement, not a request. There's no urgency behind it anymore. The need that was so apparent in her voice when I first stepped in the shower isn't there anymore. She's not yearning for my body to be in hers. Frankly, I'm not anymore either. Hearing her come and feeling the desire flow through her body is all the satisfaction I need right now. I just want to hold her. I want her to know she can trust me, with not only her body, but her secrets too.

I stand and pull her into my chest. I hold her against me as her breathing finally levels. I skim my lips across her forehead. "Do you want to get out now?"

She only nods against me in response. Her hands still cling tightly to my waist. I have to reach behind her to turn off the shower. I pull her with me. I can't let her go.

I hear the whimper before I feel it run through her. She sobs briefly, her hands moving from my waist to my chest. She taps her hands against me. "I'm sorry."

"For what?" I stroke her damp hair as we stand there, clinging to each other in the nude. "Tell me."

"I can't." There's anger woven into the response. It's not directed at me. I can sense that immediately. She's fighting with herself.

I open the door and we both recoil from the cool air that juts into the shower stall. I grab a large white towel. I wrap it around her, pulling her back into my body. "Let's get you dressed."

She shakes her head. "No. I want to go to bed."

I've lost track of time but I know it's no later than seven. She worked the lunch shift today, which means she got off at six. I left my office shortly after that. "You want to go to bed?"

"I want you to hold me."

I can't argue the point. It's exactly what I want to. I guide her out of the shower before I grab another towel. I dry every inch of her body carefully while she watches me in silence. I wrap the towel I used to soak the water from her around my own waist.

"I love you, Nathan." Her voice cracks with the words.

I pull her back into me. I rest her head against my chest. "I love you too, Jessica. I love you so much."

Chapter 15

She fell asleep almost instantly after I carried her to the bed. I've watched her sleep for more than three hours now. The only break I took was to scurry to the kitchen to grab an apple. I can't pull myself away from her. This beautiful woman that I adore more than anything on this earth is in a battle with herself. She's fighting her own demons and I've been so fucking worried that she's screwing someone else that I haven't noticed that.

The shrill bite of a cell phone cuts through the dark silence. She pushes against me before her eyes pop open. It takes a moment for her to register where she is. I see it within her expression.

"You fell asleep," I say quietly between the phone's rings. "I wanted you to sleep all night."

"Is that my phone?" She's sitting now, her gaze flowing over the darkened space.

I point towards the nightstand. "It's my phone."

"You should get it." She leans over me, her full, round breasts brushing against my chest. "It might be important."

"It's not important."

"You don't know that." She inches her reach closer to the phone. "What if it's about work?"

I grab her hand to stall it. "I don't care who it is. This is more important."
She stops and stares at me. "I'm sorry I was crying in the shower."

My hand jumps to my chest at the words. I feel an instant ache inside of me. "You're sorry for crying?" I ask. "You're sorry that you were upset? Why?"

"You have such a high pressure job." She leans back and I let go of her hand. "I don't want to add to that."

It's a weak excuse. Jessica has never been overly concerned with the stress of my work. It's not for lack of interest. She's always pressing me to work less and live more. Right now, she's using it as an excuse to hide behind her own wall of secrets. Seeing her body overcome with sadness when I got home pushed me to my breaking point. "We have to talk about what's going on."

I see her shut down right before my eyes. She's not about to start a confessional about her and the Governor. I'm going to have to rip every detail out of her with pointed questions. I get that. I see it.

"I was just having a bad day."

"You're lying." I don't see any reason to mince words. I'm not going to let her waste my time by leading down a path that has no eventual destination. She's better at diverting than I am which says a lot considering my career path.

Her reaction isn't instantaneous. She stalls before she finally speaks. "You have no right calling me a liar."

It's a weak defense. "I call it like I see it, Jessica. Don't bullshit me anymore."

Her brow pops up and in the dim light of the room I can't register anything more in her expression. "You're still hung up on Thomas talking to me, aren't you?"

If the woman knew how to shoot a gun, she'd be an expert marksman. That hit and it hurt. Her intended target, namely me, didn't even see that coming. "No. I saw him."

I wait for her reaction. It's going to tell me a lot about whether she's talked to him since this afternoon. She's horrible at disguising her true feelings. "When?"

I arch my brow. "You didn't know?"

"Know what?" She leans back on her elbows creating distance between us on the bed.

"Christ," I say under my breath. "Let's not play games."

"I'm not playing any games."

"You know exactly what I'm talking about, Jessica." I push on her forearm. "I saw Thomas. I saw him today."

She's up on her ass in an instant, the sheet falling to reveal her plump tits. "I told you I handled that. Why did you go see him?"

I level my eyes on her face. I can't stare at her ripe, beautiful body if I'm going to make any headway with this. "He came to see me."

"Why?"

I need to be at eye level with her when I discuss this so I sit up and lean my back into the heavy, wooden headboard. "He wanted me to give you a message."

Her hand bolts to pull the sheet up over her chest. She feels exposed. I can see it not only in the movement of her body, but I can hear it in how labored her breathing has suddenly become. "What message?"

I want to touch her. If I touch her, she'll know that we're connected regardless of what her asshole of an ex-lover said to me. I skim my hand along her leg. "He told me you signed an agreement."

Her head darts to the side. She stares directly at me. "That's all he said?"

I spare her the juvenile details of the Governor's need to talk about her oral skills. My skin is still on fire from that comment. "He wanted me to remind you that you signed a confidentiality agreement."

"He didn't tell you more than that?" There's a hopeful lilt to her voice that wasn't there before. I can sense the relief washing off her shoulders. She's suddenly less tense. She leans forward, letting her arms relax at her sides.

"He didn't." I lean forward too trying desperately to catch her gaze. "You're going to tell me more."

Her breathing stalls. I hear her swallow. "I'm going to tell you more?"

"You are," I say, trying not to sounds as completely impatient as I feel. "You're going to tell me exactly what he's holding over your head."

She pulls her fingers through her hair before settling them on her lap. "I can't do that." There's no defiance at all in her tone. It's a simple, stated fact.

"Why not?"

"I signed that agreement, Nathan." She tosses her legs over the side of the bed. "If I break it, he can sue me."

"I'm a fucking lawyer, Jessica." I pull on her arm stopping her in place. "You can tell me."

"I can't." She tries in vain to break free of my grasp. "I can't tell anyone."

I tug harder on her, willing her to turn and face me. "You know you can tell me. I understand the ramifications."

She only shakes her head from side-to-side with her back still turned to me. "He'll find out I told you."

"He can't." I push. "There's no fucking way he'll ever know."

She jerks her arm free of my hand. "I'm not going to tell you. I can't risk it."

I don't register the words. They only hold one meaning to me. "You don't trust me."

"It's not that." Her back is to me. "It's not about you."

The words are empty. It's the actions that are screaming at me. "If you trusted me you would fucking tell me what that asshole is holding over your head."

"I'm not talking about this." She's on her feet reaching for her robe. "You can't make me talk about this."

I pull my hand across my brow in exaggerated frustration. "I shouldn't have to make you talk about anything, Jessica. Christ, I fucking love you. I want to help you. Can't you see that?"

"You're asking me to break a promise I made." Her voice cracks as she says the words. "I can't do that."

The unspoken reference to Thomas bites into me. Is she fucking serious? Did she just say that she can't break a promise to that douchebag? "You're worried about breaking a promise you made to that son-of –a-bitch?"

"Not him." She spins around on her heel, her hair catching on the side of her face. "To myself. I promised myself I wouldn't talk about it ever."

I know I should understand. I get that I'm supposed to be the more mature one based on the fact that I'm eight years older than she is, but I can't get there. I can't wrap my brain around the fact that the woman I would give anything to won't share this secret with me. "This is killing me inside, Jessica." I bolt to my feet now too. "You're shutting me out."

"Don't make this about you." Her finger waves through the air at me. "You have secrets too."

I don't. I've laid myself bare before her. I've given her everything she's ever asked of me. I haven't held anything back. "You know everything about me, Jessica. Everything."

She shakes her head in frustration. "I don't. I don't know everything."

I'm not going to follow her down a road into the pit of my past indiscretions. I was a man whore before we met. I've admitted that. I did some stupid, reckless things when we were first together. I've owned up to all of that. I'm not going to let her drag my past back into this. "I'm not going to let you bring up my past again. It has nothing to do with this."

She freezes in place. Her eyes dart around the room. She's looking for an escape route, not in a physical sense, but an emotional one. She wants out. I see it in her expression. She wants this conversation to be over. "I can't do this right now," she whispers softly.

"I can't keep living in the dark." I reach for my own robe that I threw on a chair this morning. "I have been nothing but transparent with you, Jessica. You know everything about me. It's your turn to tell me what's going on."

"It's in the past." She takes a step towards the foot of the bed before she stops.

I move towards her. I don't want to crowd her but there's no way in hell I'm letting her out of this room. "You can trust me with anything." I need to sound as sure about this as I feel. I'm scared. I'm scared shitless that she's going to tell me something that will throw my heart out into orbit. I've never allowed myself the chance to love a woman before. This is new territory for me. I need her to trust in me, just as much as I trust in her.

"It's not that simple," she says, defeat coursing over the words. "I've never told anyone about it."

That's progress. It's a small confession but it's telling. This has been pulling at her for years. She's hidden it away from everyone.

"I can't tell you, Nathan." She lowers herself onto the corner of the bed, her back still turned to me. "I can't talk about it."

He hurt her. He hurt her in ways that have now defined her. "What did he do to you?"

"I did it to myself." Her voice is so soft. It filters into the room with a silent ease. "I made my own choices."

"I can help you." I'm around the bed now, standing in front of her. "Let me help you."

She looks up and in that instant I see a different person within her eyes. The soft, gentle soul that is always staring back at me has been replaced by a vacant shell. "No one can help me."

I'm on my knees now, my hands resting on either side of her body. "Jessica. It's me. We tell each other everything. Just fucking tell me."

Her eyes scan my face and for a brief moment her lips part. "I…" her voice trails as my cell phone starts ringing again.

I look to where it's sitting on the nightstand. It's too late for anyone to be calling unless it's an emergency. I ignore it. I have to. Nothing that anyone else has to say to me will ever be as important as this. "I need you to tell me what happened between you and him."

She turns back to look at the still ringing phone. "You should get it."

I shake my head briskly from side-to-side. "No. Jessica, listen to me."

"Get the phone."

I don't move. I wait until the ringing stops. "You're ripping my heart out. Just tell me what the fuck happened to you."

Her hand slides from her lap up my arm to my face. She cradles my cheek within her small palm. Just as she bites her bottom lip a single tear falls from her eye. "I did something bad."

I feel her pain through me. It bites into my heart. "I can help you. Just tell me."

She hesitates before leaning forward to kiss me softly on my mouth. Her lips are lush and warm. I lean into the kiss. I know she needs the physical connection to feel close to me. I need that too.

I feel lost the moment she pulls back. "It was so long ago, Nathan. I can't change any of it now."

I scoop her hand into mine and bring it to my lips. I need to kiss her still. I want to feel my lips touching her. "You don't need to change it. You can share it. It will help."

"Nothing will help." Her tone is stronger and more determined. "Nothing will ever change what I did."

She wants me to give up. I can see in her eyes that she's growing weary. I'm exhausting her with my unending assault. I need to get to the bottom of what's going on with her. I need her to tell me before this thing pulls her away from me for good. "I'm not going to give up, Jessica," I say with determined clarity. "You have to tell me."

She pulls back, her hand dropping from mine. "I can't."

"I need you to."

She taps her foot on the hardwood floor. She's restless. She's aching to bolt but I'm trapping her body with mine. It's as much to take comfort in how close we are as it is to keep her in place.

"I won't tell you."

I lean forward resting my head briefly in her lap. "You have to tell me."

I feel her fingers weave through my hair before she harshly pulls my head back up. She stares at me in silence, her eyes never wavering from mine. "You aren't listening to me, Nathan."

I'm exasperated. I can't keep running in the same circle trying to catch her. She has to give me a little. If she won't, I don't know how the two of us can move forward. "I am listening to you. We are in a relationship with each other, Jessica," I say each word with force. "I love you. I need you to be honest with me. I need you to tell me what the fuck happened between you and Thomas."

Her back tenses. I see the strength return to her face. Her chin juts up, her shoulders bolt forward and she looks me right in the eyes. "It's none of your business."

I recoil so strongly that I fall backwards. My ass hits the hardwood floor with a dull thud. I stare up at her. Her expression is empty and void of anything. I don't say a word as she stands, steps over me and walks out of the bedroom.

Chapter 16

"He died?" I repeat the question again, certain that I didn't hear the answer correctly the first time. "What do you mean he died?"

Brian, one of the junior attorneys at our firm, nods his head. "He went to take a nap and one of his granddaughters found him in bed. He was dead."

The words are so harsh and final. I just saw the man yesterday. I was in such a hurry to get him out of my office that I hadn't offered him any reassurance about his case. I didn't even bother to call him last night, after my marathon meeting. I wanted to reach out to him to give him hope. I thought I'd have time to do that today.

"I tried to call you last night to tell you but you must have gone to bed early."

It takes me a minute to register what he's saying. That was him calling. After Jessica had locked herself in the guest room I'd had a few bourbons. I didn't even bother looking at the phone at that point. I didn't give a shit about anything but my relationship, which seemed to be in free fall mode.

"Have you spoken to his granddaughters yet?" Brian's keeping the conversation moving at a forward pace all on his own.

"No," I say in a hushed tone. "I haven't talked to either of them."

"One called me this morning." He pulls out his smart phone. "I sent flowers on your behalf."

I nod. "I need a number. Give me the number of one of them."

He grazes his thumb over the screen of his phone. "I texted it to you. Her name is Pam. She's really broken up."

"Thanks," I throw the word at him. I'm not thankful. I wish that he hadn't come racing into my office the moment I arrived to dump this pile of shit on my lap. How the fuck am I supposed to handle this? I deal with death all the time. A big portion of my business focuses on people selling shares or companies after the death of someone they love. Suddenly, it all seems that much more real.

"Do you need anything?" He's hovering and it's making me completely uncomfortable. I need him to get the fuck out of my office but he's been assigned to be my assistant for the next half a year. If I make partner, I'm shifting his ass to someone else's office first thing.

"Nothing," I grumble as I wave my hand at him. "Go back to your office."

He doesn't take offense at how gruff the words are. "Call me if you need anything."

By his tone, you'd think that I'd suffered a personal loss this morning. I guess in a way I had. My girlfriend has pushed me into a corner. She's made it crystal clear that she's never going to share the secrets that have defined her past.

The ringing of my desk phone jars me back into the reality of the moment. I reach for it.

"Mr. Moore, Mr. Ryan is here."

"Let him in."

I'd called Garrett this morning on my way into the office. I'd walked. Normally I'd take the subway but I was up early and knew that both the exercise and fresh air wouldn't hurt my mood. It was a wasted effort though. After trying to weave my way through a host of tourists on Central Park South, I almost lost it. Bad moods and pedestrian traffic don't mix in my world.

"Sorry I missed your call." He walks through the open door of my office. "Do you want this shut?"

I nod. "Close it and sit down."

"You're chipper," he jokes. "What the fuck is going on with you?"

Confiding in Garrett isn't my first choice. My first choice is my sister, Sandra. When I called her this morning she wasted no time in informing me that both her kids were down with the flu. She was stressed, at her wit's end and completely preoccupied. I couldn't dump anything else into her lap.

"You sounded pissed on the phone," he continues. "Is it Jessica?"

I nod. This is the point where I tell him that I have doubts about the woman I've been begging to marry me for the past six months. I have to swallow my pride if I'm going to get his input. I need to let go and just spill it. "It's her."

"Is it about Governor Lane?" he asks, doing little to cover his know-it-all attitude. "I thought there was something going on there."

I knew this was a bad idea. What the fuck was I expecting when I called Garrett? There's no way in hell I can tell him what's going on with Jessica without him throwing it all back in my face. He's never believed we were a good fit. He knows I love her but he's told me more than once that I can do better than her. He's wrong. "We just had an argument." I try to sound nonchalant. "I overreacted when I called you."

He eyes me up from across the desk. "That's bullshit."

"Bullshit?" I crack a smile as I toss the word back at him.

"You were torn up on the phone." He taps his index finger on the edge of the desk. "You didn't call me because you two argued. It's more than that."

He's right. We both know it. The problem is that I feel like I'm betraying Jessica. I can't do that. Regardless of how much she shuts me out, I can't start sharing what's happening between us with just anyone. I can't do that to her. "It's more than that," I lie. "I lost a client this morning."

"I don't blame them," he chuckles. "I'd fire you too if you were my lawyer."

"Not fired." I shake my head. "My client died."

"Fuck." He pulls in a heavy breath. "That's rough, man."

I turn my chair so I facing the bank of windows that overlook the city. He knows Mr. Wilkinson. Garrett is the one who recommended me to him. I don't want to get into the details of his death right now. "You never know when it will be the end. One day you're making phone calls, meeting with people, and living your life and then you go to sleep and never wake up."

"How old was he?"

"Older," I toss the word behind me. "He had great grandchildren."

I hear him shift in the chair. "He lived a long life. Not everyone can say that."

"You're right," I acquiesce. Mr. Wilkinson had lived longer than most people can expect to. He lived a life that was filled with love and family. He'd worked hard to provide for the people he loved and then at the end he died with the worry that it was all stolen from him.

"What happens to his case now?"

I stare straight ahead, my eyes locked on the streams of people filling the sidewalks. Each of them has a story to tell. They've all lost people they love. I'm going to lose the person I love more than anyone if I don't fix things now. "His case?" I parrot back the words.

"Your client?" He speaks slowly and clearly. "Nate, what happens to his case now?"

I turn quickly in my chair, pulling my suit jacket back on as I stand. "I get as much as I can for his family. I don't give up until I win." The words hold much more meaning than Garrett could ever realize.

Chapter 17

"She's really kind." Her voice completely matches her appearance.

"I think so too," I say as I tip my water glass towards her.

She picks up the menu from the table. "Have you been together a long time?"

I smile at her, my name scanning over her nametag. "Not long enough, Cindy," I offer. "I wish I'd met her the day she was born."

Her hand leaps to her chest. "That's so romantic. Jess is so lucky."

"No." I purse my lips together. "I'm lucky. Can you tell me how much longer until her break?"

She leans closer. Her hand darts to the side of her mouth as if she's going to share a national secret with me and wants to ensure that no one else in the vicinity hears it. "She already had her break but she said she'll finish up and be right out to talk to you."

My heart is pounding. I haven't been this nervous to talk to Jessica since the second night I saw her at the club. The first night, I fell asleep before I took her into my bed. I went back to the club again the following night with the hope that she'd magically reappear. She did. I knew when I saw her then, that I'd never let her out of my sight again. I can't. My heart can't take it. "I'll be waiting right here."

"I'll get your sandwich." She turns on her heel and walks towards the kitchen.

I use the moment alone to look at my phone. I've tried calling Pam Wilkinson twice and there's been no response. I'm actually grateful for that. I'm not sure what I can offer in terms of condolences. I just want to reiterate to her that I'm working as hard as I can to settle her grandfather's case. I am. I need to get my focus back into work. I can only do that if Jessica and I are in a good place.

"Nathan." Her hand brushes over mine as she takes a seat across from me. "You didn't have to come here to see me."

I look up. Her blonde hair is pulled back into a tight bun. She's not wearing any make up. It only adds to how beautiful she is.

She looks young, fresh and alive. Her chef's jacket is stained with a myriad of colors. I can tell she's been working hard. She has been for months now. Between her job here and her classes at school, it's a wonder she's made any time for me at all. "You're so beautiful." I don't plan for the words to escape from me, but I can't temper them.

"I look like shit," she whispers back with a small grin. "I couldn't sleep."

"The bed in the guestroom is made of rocks." I cock a brow. "You need to stop running in there when things get rough."

She twists her lips together. "I know."

"I pushed you for a reason." I don't see any advantage in dancing around the subject. If I dive right in, she'll understand exactly where I'm coming from. "You're my life, Jessica. You're my fucking life."

Cindy reappears with a plate in hand. She places it on the table in front of me. "Can I get you anything else?" she asks, her eyes glued to me.

"This is good." I don't glance at the food at all. I can't stop staring at Jessica.

"Alright." Cindy turns quickly on her heels and disappears into the late lunch crowd that has now gathered in Axel NY.

Jessica reaches across the table towards the plate. "I'm really hungry."

I don't hesitate as I push it closer to her. "Eat. Please, Jessica, eat."

She picks up the sandwich and takes a hearty bite. It's one of the things I absolutely love about her. She's not scared shitless of food. She'll eat and eat until she's full. Her body shows it. She's voluptuous, healthy and strong. "I can't talk for long," she says between bites.

I follow her lead and take a bite of the other half of the sandwich. "Did you make this?" I nod towards the plate.

She smiles broadly. "I did."

"You're amazing." The words leave my lips with so much emotion. There's too much emotion in them. I'm talking about a fucking sandwich for Christ's sake. "I've never met anyone like you."

She dips her chin towards the table trying to mask the blush that is coursing over her face. "You always say that."

I reach across to touch her cheek. I run my index finger down her chin. "I mean it. There isn't another woman on this planet like you. There just isn't."

"I don't want this to come between us." Her eyes lock with mine. "I can't lose you, Nathan."

They're the words I've been starved for since we left her sister's wedding. "I'm not going anywhere, Jessica. I will never leave you."

"I didn't mean what I said." She leans over the table to brush her hand against mine. "I'm sorry I lashed out at you. Please forgive me."

"I already have." It's not a lie. I can't stay mad at her. I can't.

***

"Goddamn you," I say in a low tone. "Fuck, this is so good."

She doesn't flinch. Her mouth is still wrapped tightly around my cock. The moment she walked into the apartment after work, she was on top of me. "Yes," she whispers around my cock. "It's so good."

I pull harshly on her hair, guiding my cock even deeper into her throat. She can take it all. She moans at the sensation as it touches the back of her throat. I almost fucking lose it. "I need to come."

Her hands dart up to circle the thickness. She slowly pumps my dick in and out of her mouth.

"Fuck me, Jessica." I push my hips up from the mattress. "Let me fuck your mouth."

Her legs widen and I can see how wet she is. I have to taste her. As soon as I blow my load down her throat, I'm going to lick that beautiful body of hers until she comes.   "You're going to make me come so hard." The words tumble out of me in a twisted mess. My breathing is heavy and loud. I can't control the guttural moans. I can't control anything when it's like this.

She pulls back until the head of my cock pops out of her mouth. "Shoot it all into my mouth, Nathan," she purrs. "Fill me up with it."

My body takes over. My hips buck off the bed as I push on her head, directing her mouth back over my cock. I feel the first hot stream of come as it leaves my body. She moans at the taste, her tongue expertly coaxing more and more from it, until I'm still. I look down marveling at how fucking erotic she looks as she twirls her tongue over the head, lapping up every last drop.

"I need to taste you, Jessica." I motion for her to come on top of me. "Sit on my face so I can eat you."

She moves quickly, reaching forward to grab the edge of the headboard as her legs straddle my head. The sweet scent of her arousal brings my cock instantly back to life. I stare at her folds, my tongue racing over my lips. I swear I could come just from the taste of her. It's intoxicating, it's sweet and it's everything I need.

"Jesus, you're so ready." I dip my tongue inside of her and she squeals in delight. She spreads her legs farther apart giving me even more access to her core.

"Lick it there, Nathan," she says in a breathless tone. "Ah, yes, just like that."

I take her lead and lap my tongue over her clit. I hold tight to her thighs as she rides my face. Her body gives in to all the pleasure. Her hips rock back and forth quickly and urgently as she races to find her release.

"I'm so close." I don't need to hear the words. I can feel it. I can sense it in the way her legs are moving. I can hear it in her breathing.

I lick faster and harder. I move my head to match the rhythm of my tongue. I could eat her sweet pussy for hours and never tire of it. This is my heaven. This is the woman I'm supposed to spend my forever with.

Her body tilts back as an orgasms captures her. Her hands hold tightly to the headboard. I look up. Her beautiful big tits are bouncing heavily with the weight of her arousal. She allows the orgasm to carry her. She rides the wave until it's over.

"I can't believe how good that felt." She moves her legs pulling her body away from my mouth. "It's always so good, Nathan."

I smile at the compliment. "I love that, Jessica. I can't tell you what it's like to eat you like that."

She settles next to me on the bed. "You like it?"

"I fucking love it." I pull her into my chest. "You have such a sweet body. I love the taste of it."

She sighs deeply as she pulls her arm around my waist. "I've missed this. I've missed us."

I kiss the top of her head softly. "I hate it when we aren't close." It's more than that though. It's not just about the sex. I hate it when there's anything dividing our hearts. I can't function. I'm lost when I feel as though Jessica's drifted away from me.

"I've felt really alone."

I pull back so I can look at her face. There's a sadness sweeping over it. "You're never alone. I'm always here. Always."

Chapter 18

"You've been mad at me," she whispers. They're the words you'd expect an impish child to say to their parent. We never speak about our age difference, but there's an unspoken understanding that she views me as someone who will take care of her. She sees me as the one who guides her in some ways, and I've tried my best to live up to that.

"I haven't been mad at you," I correct her with a soft stroke on her bare back with my fingers. "I've been mad at the situation."

"You mean the situation with Thomas?" she says his name with such effortless ease that it drives straight through me. I don't want her to bring him up at every turn. I can't stand the sound of his name.

"Yes," I don't offer more.

"It's very complicated." She taps her hand on my chest before her finger circles a path around my nipple.

"I'm really good with complicated things, Jessica." I pull her hand into mine. "I've shared every secret I have with you because you wanted that."

She nods and her hair pulls across my skin. "I needed that from you."

It's the opening I've been waiting impatiently for. "I need that from you too."

"What happens if I break the confidentiality agreement?" She pulls herself up onto her elbows on my chest so she's looking directly at my face. "What will happen to me?"

"Nothing." I tuck a piece of hair behind her ear. "I'm an attorney, I won't tell anyone."

"What about the money?"

I wait for more but that's the end of the question. Money? What fucking money is she talking about? "What money, Jessica?"

Her fingers pull on the bottom of her hair in a thoughtless, nervous gesture. "The money I got when I signed the form."

She sounds simple and naïve. I can't tell if she's doing it on purpose or if there's a genuine question behind her words. "Is that part of the confidentiality agreement you signed? You're not supposed to tell people you were paid?"

"I guess." She shrugs her shoulders. "The lawyer that Thomas had said I couldn't talk about it with anyone or they'd need the money back."

That fucking asshole threatened her. He threatened her so she'd keep her mouth shut about the affair. "How much money was it?" The amount is inconsequential. I don't give a fuck about it. I want to know how much he thought her silence was worth.

"It was a lot of money." She looks up into the air. "I've never told anyone about this."

I can see how pained she is by sharing all of it. I know that it's wearing her down inside. "You can tell me."

"Nathan." Her hand juts to my chin. "I'm not a bad person."

I see through the tears that are now clouding her eyes. I see the conflict that is pulling her apart from the inside out. "You're the best person I know."

"I wish that were true." Her voice breaks with a sob. "I should have been a better person then. I was young."

It's a telling confession. She rode my ass so hard when we first met about the life I'd had before we met. This is the first time I've heard her talk about her own shortcomings. Other than the brief moment in time when she blamed herself for Josh's grandfather's death, I've never seen Jessica crack like this. "We all make mistakes."

"Your mistakes were nothing like mine." She pushes closer towards me. "I'm way worse than you."

I smile at the proclamation. I've worked hard to change who I am. Before I met Jessica I'd think nothing of picking a woman up with a drink, fucking her senseless and then sending her home, without even knowing her name. I'd rarely think of the women I was with after they walked out of my hotel suite. I was an asshole. I used them for my own selfish pleasure. "I'm trying to be a better person."

Her eyes catch mine. "I didn't mean it like that."

"I know."

"I met Thomas the summer after I graduated from high school." She stares directly at me. "I was eighteen. He was a lot older than me."

I nod. I don't know his exact age. It doesn't matter. I just know that he was too old for her when she was that young. She had to have been even more fragile than she is now. "Where did you meet?"

"I worked in his campaign office." She pulls her hand across my chest. "It was a summer job and I needed the money."

"His office was in Bloomfield?" It's a small town. I didn't realize exactly how small until I went to the wedding. It's hard to imagine any senator setting up shop in a ghost town like that.

"No," she pauses before she continues. "It was in Greenwich."

I had no idea that she spent time away from home after high school. We've never talked about that time in either of our lives. I instantly regret that. "You went there to work?"

She nods and her chin hits my chest with each movement. "My friends were renting a house there for the summer. I couldn't afford to go without a job in place, so I asked around and someone told me Thomas was looking for help."

It was so innocent. She only wanted the chance to spend a summer away with her friends. Who knew that she'd end up in the bed of the man who hired her to work for him? "Did you work for him the entire summer?"

"I did." She blows out a breath. "I went to school in the fall but we still kept in touch."

Kept in touch? She means they fucked right through the fall semester. "When did it end?"

"Around the holidays." She closes her eyes briefly. "I went home to see my mother and a lot changed then."

"Like what?" I don't want to sound insensitive but I'm hearing about a relationship that has completely defined the woman I care for. I want to skip past all the inconsequential details and dive right into the part about why she had to sign a confidentiality agreement.

She stops and stares past me to the headboard. Her lips open slightly and her breathing increases. "My mother had cancer. She was diagnosed right before the holidays."

It's the first I've heard of it. Judging by the way her mother was fondling me; I'd say she's recovered nicely. "Cancer?"

"Breast cancer," she clarifies. "She needed a double mastectomy."

"Christ, Jessica." I run my hand down her back. "I didn't know."

She shivers slightly. "We don't talk about it. She doesn't like us to talk about it."

It's hard to imagine a teenage girl being thrown into the middle of a medical mess like that. "I'm sorry, Jessica. That's a lot to deal with."

"It was." Her eyes dart back to my face. "My sister was away. She went to school on the west coast. She didn't come back for the surgery."

"You had to take care of your mother alone?"

Her eyebrows pull together. I can tell she's remembering what she felt back then. "My grandmother helped but she wasn't that well either. I skipped a semester to stay home to help."

"You had to sacrifice a lot." The words aren't meant as a compliment. They're simply a statement. It's the truth. It's obvious that she had to give up part of her life to help her mother.

Her eyes settle on my mouth as she runs the pad of her thumb over my bottom lip. "She's my mother. I had to."

I want to push back to the point where she talked about Thomas but I can't. I can't tear her away from this. "She's okay now?" It's a question not based in actual concern. I saw for myself just how well her mother was. I want Jessica to acknowledge it too.

"She's fine." A small smile pulls at the corner of her mouth. "She went through treatment and came out fine. She's been cancer free since."

The pieces of the puzzle aren't falling together the way they should. She's telling me that she nursed her mother back to health after a cancer scare. She shared that she missed a semester of school to care for her and yet they don't get along. There was not an ounce of closeness between them at the wedding.

"I'm glad she's okay," I offer mostly because I don't know what the hell to say.

"I had to hire a nurse to take care of her. I couldn't do it on my own." She doesn't meet my gaze. "I used the money for that."

"The money you got from signing the agreement?"

"Yes." She pushes her face against my chest. "I used that money."

"What was the agreement about?" I know that she wants me to drop it. I know that I should. "Did you agree to not talk about the affair? Is that what it was?" I already know that's not it. Judging by the careless way Thomas talked about Jessica blowing him, I'd venture a guess that she wasn't his only indiscretion.

"No." Her head flies back up. "He had so many affairs."

I take comfort in the confirmation even though I know it must sting her to carry that knowledge. "What was it about then?"

She hesitates before pushing her body against mine. I can feel every crevice of her form. The softness of her breasts caresses my side, the wetness of her core touches my hip as she pulls her leg over me. "You'll stop loving me, Nathan."

I don't cry. It's not something that comes naturally to me. It's not that I'm a cold and insensitive bastard. I just don't feel things as deeply as others do. I know that. I've always known that. "Nothing you could say to me would make me stop loving you, Jessica. Nothing." I feel the tears building within me.

She sobs slightly. "This will."

"I promise it won't." I try to contain my emotions. I'm so close to understanding the pain that she's been carrying with her for years.

"I'm a good person." She nods her head up and down against me.

"You're a remarkable person," I assure her with a kiss to the forehead. "You're the most amazing person I've ever known."

"I would change it if I could," she whispers into my chest. "I would change it all if I could."

I pull my hand across her cheek, cupping her face. I wipe away the constant stream of tears. "Tell me, Jessica."

"I think about it every day." Her voice is calm and controlled now. "I cry every day."

My heart is breaking for her. I can literally feel the pain in her heart seeping into mine. She's broken. She's tortured. This woman has been carrying a burden that is pulling the life out of her. Thomas just brought it all to the surface again. "Share it with me, Jessica. I'll help you. I will."

"I gave her to him." She pulls a deep breath in as the tears flow again. "I just gave her to him."

I close my eyes. I feel my lungs collapse under the weight of the words. I have to ask although my heart already knows. "Who did you give to him?"

"I gave him my daughter."

Chapter 19

"Please tell me you don't hate me." She's on her knees on the floor by the bed.

I drop next to her. I had to leave the room to regain control of my own emotions after her confession. My heart broke in two hearing her tell me about her daughter. Jessica has a daughter. Jessica is someone's mother. "I love you, Jessica." I wrap my hands around her face, cupping her cheeks in my hands. "Never question that."

"I hate myself." She tries to hang her head down but my grip is too strong.

"You can't do this to yourself." I kiss the tip of her nose. "You made a decision at the time that was right for you." I mean the words. She was young and overwhelmed.

She nods but there's no conviction behind it at all. "I try not to think about her too much. I can't. It hurts." Her hand leaps to her chest.

"You can't think about it." I want to reassure her. I want her to believe that she did what was best for both her and her daughter.

She scans my eyes with her own. "I asked Thomas about her at the wedding."

"That's why he flipped out?" I run the pad of my thumb over her cheek. "What did you ask him?"

She shrugs her shoulders. "I just wanted to know what she was like. I asked if she was happy."

It's pure Jessica. It's natural that she'd asked. I can't imagine her not caring about a child she gave birth to. "What did he say?"

"He told me to mind my own fucking business."

My shoulders tense at the words. Thomas is such a fucked up piece of shit. "Why was he even there?"

"At Julie's wedding?"

I nod. "Does he even know your sister?"

She bites the edge of her bottom lip. "He knows her husband. There's some business connection there."

"I wish you would have told me about him that night, Jessica," I say softly. I don't want to sound like an asshole. She just confessed to having a child with another man and I'm riding her ass about not telling me about it. I can see how it's broken her.

"Do you remember when I found out about you and Cassandra?"

Cassie's name comes out of left field. I take a moment to register it. "When she brought you to my apartment?"

She pulls her hand across her face before it settles over my fingers. "No. It was later. It was the day you told me about how you dated her because of the twins."

I remember that conversation. When I met Cassandra I was looking to settle down. The fact that she had two toddlers was enough of a pull for me to give up having one night stands. I loved her kids. I spent hours just hanging out with them. If I could have forged a relationship with them, and left Cassie out of the equation, I would have done that. "Yes, I remember that."

"I almost told you about my daughter that day."

"Why didn't you?" I try to sound sympathetic and understanding. The truth is that I'm still reeling from the news that Jessica had a child. How have I loved her for this long and been completely unaware of that?

She etches an invisible line along my top lip with her finger. "You want to be a dad."

It's a statement that doesn't surprise me at all. It's true. I've been dropping hints for months about wanting to have a baby with Jessica. "I do want that."

"I thought that if I…well, I imagined…" she stammers.

"You thought that if you told me you gave up a child that I'd go looking for someone else?" The notion behind the words is crueler than they sound. "Did you really believe that?"

"Drew." Her eyes fill with tears again. "I didn't tell you because of what you said to Drew that day."

The conversation is flying around so many curves that I can barely keep up. "Drew? What are you talking about?"

"The night I saw you at the bar with him," she hesitates with a deep breath. "That night I punched him. You remember that night?"

I nod. How could I forget? I watched all five feet two inches of her deck a guy a foot taller than her. "I'll never forget that night."

"Neither will I." Her gaze is steady and measured. "That's the night you told Drew he was a horrible excuse for a parent because he abandoned his kids."

I can't think right now. I try to push my memory back to that night but I've blocked out most of it. I hurt Jessica so much that night. I ripped her heart out and threw it against the floor. It had taken months to get her to trust me again after that. There's no way in hell I can remember exactly what I said to Drew. "That wasn't about you. That was about Drew."

"I heard you tell him that he wasn't taking care of his kids."

"Jesus, Jessica." I run my fingers over her cheeks. "That was about him. He was gambling away everything. He wasn't taking care of his own children. Cassie was struggling to make it on her own with those two kids."

"Exactly." She pushes my hands away. "I haven't taken care of my own child either."

Trying to reason with her isn't going to work. There's no way in hell I could have known that she gave her child to its father when I said those things about Drew. "Jessica, listen to me."

"I'm listening," she says with little emotion. "I've always listened to you. I've watched you." She's on her feet now.

I pull myself up and sit on the edge of the bed. "What do you mean you've watched me?"

"I've watched you with your niece and nephew. I see how much you love them." She lowers herself next to me on the bed. "You would have loved her too, Nathan. You would have loved my daughter too."

Regret. It's there washing over her like a tidal wave. It's not just about the fact that she wishes she would have kept her child. It's more than that. It's about the family we could have already been.

"If I had her with me when we met, you would have loved her too, wouldn't you?"

I can't lie to her. I promised her that when we first met. "Yes, Jessica. I would have loved her too."

She's back on her feet. I don't stop her as she races down the hallway, slamming the washroom door behind her.

Chapter 20

"I'd like to see the contract." I stand next to the bed. I'd gone to work in my home office while she was in the washroom. I know when Jessica needs space. I give it to her. I can't take that away from her.

She doesn't turn to look at me. "I have it somewhere. I guess I can find it."

"It's important." My leg twitches. I want to climb into the bed next to her. I want to wrap my arms and legs around her. I want to pull her into my chest and never let her go.

She flips over in one easy movement. "Why is it important?"

I'm not going to give her any false hope. Naturally, my mind jumped to the validity of the agreement. I need to know if she gave up all of her parental rights. I need to know if the contract she signed is legal and binding. I need to know if that little girl who is a part of the woman I love is happy in the home she's living in.

"Nathan, tell me why you need to see it."

"I'm a lawyer, Jessica." I slide under the sheet. "I have to look it over."

I see the defeat in her eyes. She was looking for something more. She has to know that even if there's a loophole that deems the agreement null and void that ripping a six-year-old child away from her family has far reaching consequences.

"I'll look for it tomorrow." She turns back around. "I haven't looked at it since I signed it."

I nod as I hold tightly to her body. "Thank you, Jessica."

"For what?" She cranes her neck to the side. "Why are you thanking me?"

"Thank you," I begin as I tap my hand against her chest. "Thank you for finally letting me in here."

***

"Pam," I say her name as if we've been friends for years. Based on the hug she gave me when she came barreling into my office earlier, it feels like we've known each other for a lifetime. "I'm very close to a settlement now."

"My grandfather would be happy." She clasps her hands together in her lap.

"He was a great guy," I offer. Since Mr. Wilkinson had died, I'd been fighting with Anthony Mercado's counsel to come to an agreement. I was glad for the distraction. Jessica had thrown herself full force back into her school work and her job at Axel NY. I knew that it was a coping tool. She was trying to drown out the knowledge that she's never had a relationship with her daughter. We've only spoken briefly about it once since that night. She explained in pained detail that her mother is constantly reminding her of how she stole her only grandchild away from her. Now, the emotional distance that I saw when I was in Bloomfield makes perfect sense.

"He spoke very highly of you, Mr. Moore."

"It's Nate," I offer. I don't want anyone to call me Nathan but Jessica. I love the way my name sounds when she says it. It fuels a part of me that I never knew existed until I met her. "That's hard to imagine, "I chuckle. "He never seemed very impressed with me."

"Really?" There's genuine surprise in the question. "He talked about you a lot. He said your work ethic is amazing."

I'm beginning to wonder if she doesn't understand the meaning of sarcasm. I can picture Mr. Wilkinson having dinner with his granddaughters as he grumbles on about what a great guy I am, all the while seething because I ignored all twenty five of his phone calls that day. "He was pretty amazing himself."

"I couldn't have asked for a better grandfather." She smiles softly. "He always said that he was specially chosen to be my granddad."

"That's lovely," I grin. "I'm hoping one day I can be the type of grandfather he was."

"He practically adopted me and my sister after our mother died."

"Your mother died?"

"When I was young," she says in a muted tone. "It was an overdose. It was accidental they said."

I don't know how to respond other than with what's expected. "I'm sorry."

"Granddad wasted no time taking us in." She folds her left hand over the right in her lap. "It was an easy transition for us. He lived next door with his wife so we just took our pillows and clothing and moved in."

"You moved in with him and your grandmother?"

"Yes," she chuckles softly. "I mean no."

I cock a brow. "I'm not following."

"She never thought of us as her grandchildren." She waves her hand through the air. "She never really paid us much mind."

"Your grandmother didn't consider you her grandchildren?"

"Granddad didn't explain this to you?" She tilts her head to the side. "You don't know, do you?"

I don't know much of anything lately it seems. "He explained that you and your sister were close to him," I offer as a starting point. I obviously need her to fill in many of the blanks.

"We lived next door to him and his wife when we were children."

I don't interrupt. I only nod, encouraging her to continue.

"He was our neighbor. He and his wife didn't have any children."

Wait. What? "Your mother wasn't his daughter?"

"No." Her tone is firm. "She lived in the house with our dad until he took off."

"Mr. Wilkinson was your neighbor?"

She sighs deeply. "He was that to begin with. Then he became our granddad. We loved him so much."

I meet her eyes with my own. "He loved you a lot too. He told me as much."

"He always said that families aren't about blood. They're about love." She tips her chin down with the words. "I was lucky to have him."

"He was lucky to have you too."

Chapter 21

"Nathan?"

"Yes?" My head darts up from the desk in my home office. "Do you need something, Jessica?"

"Are you busy?" Her eyes move from my face to the screen of my laptop.

I slam it shut with one quick flip of my wrist. "I'm never too busy for you."

"You're charming." She smiles at me from the doorway.

I smile back relishing in how beautiful she looks wearing tattered sweat pants and one of my football jerseys. Her hair is pulled into a high ponytail on her head. "Tell me what I can do for you."

She cocks a brow. "I wouldn't even know where to start with that."

I run my tongue over my bottom lip. I haven't made love with her for days. The last time was when I ate her out before she confessed everything to me. I want her so badly. I ache for her touch but I want her to heal. I want her to feel strong enough to share herself with me in every way. "You know I'll do whatever you want me to do to your body."

"That hasn't changed?"

I can't digest the question. "What do you mean?"

"You don't want me any less now that you know?" Her gaze falls to her bare feet.

"That I know that you're a mother?"

"Yes," she whispers under her breath. "You haven't tried to fuck me since that night."

"Jessica." Her name escapes me in a breathless whisper as I rise from my chair. "My body aches for your body every minute of the day. That will never change."

Her brow furrows slightly at my response. "I felt like everything was different."

"Why?" I take a few strong strides across the room until I'm standing directly in front of her. "Why would you feel that?"

"You've been so quiet." Her hands reach for the collar of my shirt. "You've come into your office every night to work."

"It's been an adjustment for us both." My hands circle her waist. "My feelings haven't changed at all. I think I love you more actually."

"More?" She dips her head to catch my gaze. "How can you love me more?"

"I don't think I can explain it."

"You can try," she counters. "Please try."

I can sense how important this is to her. She needs to find comfort in my love for her. She tore herself open emotionally for me a few days ago. I have to show her that it was worth it. I need her to see that I cherish and love her even more now.

I reach up to tap her on the tip of her nose. "The Jessica I fell in love with has a beautiful heart."

"I like that you think that."

"I don't think it, Jessica. It's the truth," I say, my eyes focused on hers. "You never gave up on me."

"I would never give up on you." Her hand drops to my chest. "I can't, Nathan."

I pull her hand into mine. "I saw something in you that I've never seen in anyone before." The inference is any other woman. We both know it. I don't have to tell her. She understands that in my eyes, there isn't another woman walking this planet that compares to her.

"You still see that now?"

I reach forward and graze my lips over hers. "When you told me about your baby… I mean your daughter," I stammer. "When you told me about her I saw a part of you that I didn't even know was there."

"What part?" Her hands grip tightly to the front of my shirt.

"You're so fucking strong." I smile. "You're the strongest person I've ever met."

"I'm not strong." She slaps her hands across my chest. "I'm not strong at all."

"I had this client, Jessica." I tilt her head up so she's looking directly at me. "He was an older man. He died recently."

"I'm sorry," she says it without an ounce of pretense. There's compassion woven deeply into it.

I nod in response. "He had two granddaughters."

"Are they young?"

"Your age," I offer. "They're both in their twenties."

She smiles at the gentle reminder of the gap in our ages. "They're not old like you?"

I wink at her before I pull my brows together in mock anger. "No. They're not old like me."

"I'm sorry they lost their grandfather."

"He loved them both very much even though he wasn't their grandfather by birth." I want this to sound gentle and I want it to bring her comfort.

"What do you mean?" She cocks her head to the side. "They were adopted?"

"He was their foster father." I kiss her forehead lightly. "He never formally adopted them, but he took them in and cared for them when their mother died."

"They were a family," she says with understanding in her eyes.

"Two nights ago when I came home you were on my laptop." I gesture behind me with my hand. "I know you closed it when you heard me come through the door."

She doesn't show any surprise at all. "Yes. I was looking at something."

I pull in a heavy breath. "You were reading about her."

Her eyes fill with tears. "I was." She nods quickly. "I wanted to know more."

"What did you learn?" I push because I have to. I need her to share. I don't want her to carry the guilt of this around with her forever.

"Her name is Jenna." She closes her eyes tightly as tears stream down her face. "She loves horses."

"She's beautiful," I offer. I had to close my office door after reading the article that popped up on my laptop screen when I opened it after Jessica went to bed. It was a profile of the Governor's family. An entire paragraph was dedicated to Jenna Lane. She's a beautiful blonde haired, blue eyed six-year-old girl. The little girl bears an unmistakable resemblance to Jessica.

"She looks like me." A ghost of a smile trails over her mouth. "She's pretty."

"She's beautiful." I whisper into her forehead. "She's really beautiful."

She nods through the tears. "She's happy."

I thought the same thing as I read the article. The smile on her face was filled with pure joy. When the reporter who wrote the piece asked what Jenna's favorite thing was she responded that it was her younger brother. She's part of a family who loves her deeply and unconditionally. "I felt that too."

"I just wish I could see her once." She fights to hold back the tears. "I never got to hold her or hug her or anything."

The words tear through me. I had no idea the baby was taken from her that quickly. "I'm sorry. I wish I could change that."

"She's where she belongs." Her shoulders tremble was she says the words. "She's part of their family now."

"She is," I whisper back. Jenna is part of their family and Jessica is mine.

Chapter 22

"Will you marry me?"

I almost fall out of my chair. "What did you say?"

She pulls in a deep breath before she slams my office door behind her. "I asked if you would marry me."

I fumble for my suit jacket. I had tossed it over the back of my chair when I got into my office this morning. I had a full morning of calls and meetings related to the Wilkinson case. If all goes according to the settlement I've worked so hard to achieve, the granddaughters will begin receiving payments within the next three months. "I have to find the ring."

"You have a ring?" Jessica pulls her hand up to her chest in mock surprise.

"I've had a ring for the last six months." I push my hand into one pocket and I come up empty. "Where the fuck did I put that goddamn ring?"

"This is romantic." She taps her finger against the desk. "I can't have this be my memory of our engagement."

"You just asked me to marry you, Jessica." I'm on my feet now. "You can't take it back. Fuck, please don't take it back."

"I'm going to walk back out the door and get the secretary to announce that I'm here." She points at my office door. "She'll call me Ms. Ross but go with it. When I come back in, you'll have the ring in your hand and you'll get down on one knee and say something romantic."

I scrub my hand across my face. "What? Did you just give me a play-by-play on how to propose to you?"

"I did." She nods. "Do you have it? Do you know what to do?"

"No." I start towards her as she nears the door. "It's not happening like this."

She tries to pull open the door but my hand holds it closed. "Nathan," she practically screams my name. "I have to get to class soon. I don't have time for this. Let me leave so I can come back and you can propose."

I smile down at her, soaking in her obvious frustration. "It's not happening, Jessica. You don't get to control this."

"I'm going to say yes if you ask me today." She stomps her heel on the floor.

"You're going to say yes when I ask you and that's not going to be today."

She taps me on the tip of my nose, turns towards the door, throws it open and walks towards the bank of elevators without turning back around.

***

"I'm here as a client, not as an attorney." I toss the agreement Jessica gave me across the desk of my friend, Lyle Benson. "You're the family law expert. Tell me what you think."

He picks the papers up and scans them quickly. "This is the case you told me about on the phone?"

"I crossed out all the names." I had painstakingly spent last night copying every page of the document before crossing out the names. I trust Lyle but the last thing I need is a leak to the press. Jessica doesn't need her name dragged into anything to do with the Governor and his family.

He tosses the papers to the side. "Give me a day or two to go over this."

"I don't have that much time," I lie. I have all the time in the world. I've studied those documents for hours. I can't find even the smallest loophole. I don't even know what is driving my incessant need to find some way for Jessica to have a role in her daughter's life. I can only attribute it to my need to give her anything she craves.

"Sit." He motions to a couch against the wall near his desk. "Give me ten minutes."

I don't normally acquiesce this easily, but for Jessica I'll hang upside down if need be. I walk slowly to the couch, lower myself down and pray that there's something in those documents that will give her the chance she wants to see her baby girl.

Chapter 23

"I'll be done school in a few weeks." She settles down on my lap on the couch.

I push my phone to the side as I pull my arms around her. "I know. I'm excited to have my girl back." The words could be interpreted as selfish. They're not. I'm Jessica's biggest supporter. I pushed her to enroll in culinary school. I give her all the space she needs to focus on her career. Cooking is her passion. I want her to excel at it. I want her to have everything in life that she desires. I'll sacrifice whatever I can to give that to her.

"You're excited that I'll have more time to suck your cock."

I laugh out loud at how brash the words are. "You're starting to sound more and more like me every day." She is. She's so open about her desire for me, just as I am with her. We talk easily and comfortably about sex. We always have. It's just one part of our relationship that I cherish deeply.

"You can't deny it, Mr. Moore." She traces a path along my chin with her lips. "You love it when I slide your big, beautiful cock between my lips."

I grab her head, tilting it to the side so I can slide my lips effortlessly over hers. I push between them with my tongue, pulling it alongside hers before I bite her bottom lip sharply. "You want me to fuck your mouth right now, don't you?"

"No." She pulls back slightly so she can work on the buttons of my shirt. "I want you to lick me until I come."

I wrap my hand around her waist and flip us over with little effort. She's laid out before me on the couch now, her beautiful body wrapped in a simple black dress. She'd teased me endlessly through dinner earlier, leaning forward so I could catch a glimpse of the side of her round breast. "You want me to eat your beautiful pussy until you come all over my face, don't you?"

She nods slowly. "Do it now."

I pull on the sash of her dress, pushing it apart. She looks magnificent, sprawled out before me in a black bra and matching panties. "I love your tits."

Her brow furrows for a moment as she watches my hands unlatch the front of her bra. Her tits fall out. They're perfectly shaped, the nipples already hardening at the promise of an orgasm.

"I want you to lick me," she says, almost begging.

"I will." I grab both of her breasts, kneading the milky flesh in my hands. "I need to bite your nipples first."

A moan escapes her before my lips even touch her skin. I race my tongue around her right nipple, pulling it to full attention. I blow on it, watching its natural reaction to the burst of chilled air.

Her hands pull on my shoulders. "I'm so aroused, Nathan."

It's a confession she doesn't need to make. Her entire body is trembling. She's aching to come. I need her to yearn for it. I want her to feel every single bite of pleasure course through her before she tumbles over the edge. "You'll come, Jessica. When I want you to come, you will."

She curses under her breath before I feel her relax beneath my touch. I lick a path towards her left breast before I bite hard on her nipple. I'm rewarded with a deep, low moan.

"You like that, don't you?" I growl. "You like when I bite your beautiful nipples."

"I do," she murmurs. "I love it."

I pull my lips across her stomach, relishing in how soft her skin is. The natural fragrance of her body consumes me. It makes me instantly hard. My cock is straining for its own release against my pants. I can't think about it. All I can focus on is how sweet she's going to taste when I lick my tongue over her hot folds.

"Lick me, please."

I love when she's like this. I can't stand how good it feels to know that she wants me as desperately as I want her. "I love how you taste. You're so sweet. You're so fucking good, Jessica."

Her hand pulls on my hair, trying to guide my face down. I lick her thigh, my face rubbing along her panties. She whimpers at the intimate touch.

"You're going to come so hard. You're going to come so hard all over my face." The words spill out of me. I can't control them.

"Do it," she coaxes. "Please, now."

I don't hesitate a moment longer. I pull her panties down and off, tossing them over my shoulder. I quickly push her legs apart while I stare down at her glistening wetness. She's so ripe and ready. Her body needs mine so desperately.

"Fuck," she draws the word across her lips slowly and softly.

I lick her hard, lapping up everything she's already offered to me. I crave the taste. "This is so good."

"So good," she parrots back as her hands weave between the strands of my hair. "Make me come."

I cup her ass in my hands as I eat her hard. I pull her clit into my mouth, holding tight to her body as she wiggles beneath me. I push a finger into her, then another. I keep up the pace, slowly fucking her with my hand as my tongue flicks her clit over and over again. I bend my finger into her, honing in on the one spot that throws her over the edge quickly and desperately.

She pulls hard on my hair as she orgasms. Her desire flows out and onto my lips. I moan at the sweetness. I lap at her folds, trying to capture every last drop that her body has gifted me with.

I still and rest my cheek against her thigh. "You're so fucking hot, Jessica, "I say into her skin. "Jesus, you don't even know how good you taste."

"Let me suck you off." Her hands flail in the air trying desperately to reach my shoulders. "I want to feel that."

"No." I crawl over her body, slowly and methodically. I stop to kiss each of her nipples I push her thighs apart, making room for my knees. "I'm going to fuck you, Jessica. I need to feel my cock inside of you."

"Oh, God."

I don't waste time removing my shirt. I can't. I need to be inside of her right now. I undo my belt before I pull the zipper of my pants down. "You're so ready."

She nods in response, her hands pulling on my shoulders. "Now."

"Now," I repeat back as I drive my cock into her balls deep. I groan loudly at the instant pleasure that races through my entire body.

"Fuck, yes," she whispers. Her hips involuntarily rise from the couch, coaxing me to start my tender assault. Her hands leap to my ass. "Fuck me hard."

I still. "No, Jessica."

"No?" Her lips race over my cheek before they find my mouth. She kisses me deep and hard, savoring in her own taste that is still lingering on my breath.

I pull back from the kiss. "I'll blow my load if you move. I can't stand how good this feels."

She moans at the words. "You like fucking me?"

I laugh at how understated that is. "I fucking love it."

"I want to come again."

"I'll eat you again."

"No." She rests her hands on my shoulders. "Don't move."

"My cock fills you up." I love the sound of the words. I love knowing how aroused she is by my body. I doubt it can compare to how I feel about hers, but I need to hear it. I want to know that I'm all she ever wants.

"It's so big." She wiggles her eyebrows. "You have such a big cock."

I laugh at the proclamation. "It's all you want."

"Forever." She sighs as she clenches her taut, wet sex around me.

"Jesus, Jessica." My breathing stalls. "I'm going to come if you keep that up."

She shifts her hips slightly. "I want you to fuck me hard, Nathan. Show me how badly you want me."

I rally back on my heels at the request. I grab tightly to her hips as I push my cock as deeply into her as it will go.

She screams slightly at the mix of pain and pleasure. "Don't stop, Nathan."

"I can't." I move faster, finding my rhythm, pounding myself into her over and over again. "I'm going to make you come so fucking hard."

She raises her hands above her head so her tits are on full display. I stare down at her face and her gorgeous body as I fuck her hard and fast. "I'll never stop this," I spit the words out between thrusts. "You're it for me, Jessica. I'll never get enough of you."

"Promise me," she grunts. "Promise."

"I'm yours." I push hard into her as I find my own sweet release within her body.

Chapter 24

"I want us to talk about something." I sit down next to her on the bed.

She pushes the button on the remote to turn off the television before she places it on her lap. "Don't do it now."

"What?"

"Don't propose right now." She taps her hand onto the sheet. "I look like shit and I don't want to remember it like this."

I can't hold in a smile. "You look gorgeous." She does. After I'd fucked her, I carried her into the bedroom and put her beneath the sheets. Then I grabbed a quick shower and a glass of bourbon while I rallied my mind around the words I need to say to her.

"Please not now." Her finger touches my knee. "Maybe you can ask tomorrow."

"It's not about that." I inch forward so I can cradle her hand in my own. "It's about something else."

"Did you make partner?" The giddiness in her tone is infectious. We haven't talked about my work in days. I know that they'll be making a decision about the partnership within the next two days. I have high hopes. I want it more than I'm willing to admit.

"Not yet." I kiss her palm. "I'll call you about that as soon as I know."

She squeezes my hands in hers. "Promise?"

"I always tell you everything right away, Jessica." I do. Well, almost everything. I haven't told her about the agreement yet. She hasn't brought it up.

She relaxes her grip on my hand. "What's it about then?"

"I took that agreement you signed to an attorney friend of mine." I steel myself for her inevitable reaction.

"No, you didn't do that." Denial. It's not what I expected, but I'll take it over anger.

"I did." I see no reason to edge around this. I did it for her. I did it with the hope that one day she'd get to stand in front of her daughter and see her precious face in person.

She pulls her hands together. I watch in silence as she traces her left thumb nail over the right. "There's no hope, is there?"

I have to tell her now. This is the moment in time when I confess to her. "Do you want to see her, Jessica?"

Her eyes fill instantly with tears. Her bottom lip quivers slightly. "I want to see her more than anything."

"It would only be once." I hold steadfast to her hand. "You can see her one time and you can't tell her who you are."

Her entire body rocks forward. The sobs overwhelm her. "I want that. Please, please let me have that."

***

"I don't understand how you made it happen." Her hand is holding so tightly to mine that I wonder if all honesty if she's going to break my fingers.

I don't want to explain all the pointed details to her. Blackmail isn't my thing. Legally it can't be my thing. I could lose my license to practice law for this stunt but I knew that the Governor would give me what I wanted. "I called Thomas after my friend reviewed the agreement. He agreed to this one meeting." I don't offer more. I can't.

"I can't thank you enough for this." She pulls in a heavy breath before her hand drops from mine. I watch in silence as she plays with the buttons on the simple white dress she chose to wear.

"I wanted you to have this, Jessica." I had. After learning that there was nothing in the agreement that would give Jessica access to her daughter, I took matters into my own hands. I called the Governor, and taped our conversation. He confessed to everything with Jessica. He couldn't shut his fucking mouth about how good she was in bed and how he'd trade his wife in for her. All I had to do was play that back to him an hour later.

"Does she know her mother isn't her mother?" Her brow rises with the question. "I mean…you know what I mean."

I wrap my arm around her shoulder. "She has no idea."

She nods slowly. I can see the information sinking in. "I can't say anything to her about who I am?" It's the same question she's asked me seven times since we left our apartment to come to the Museum of Modern Art.

"Thomas will introduce us both as old friends," I say as I adjust the collar of her dress. "If you don't feel strong enough, you squeeze my hand and we'll leave."

"No." She shakes her head. "I won't do that. I'm strong."

She's remarkably strong. It's taking every small bit of strength that she carries within her to do this. She understands completely that this may be the only time she'll speak to her daughter in her lifetime. She gets that. Yet, she's found the courage to do this. I've told her over and over again how much I admire her. I do. She's stronger than I can ever hope to be.

"They'll be here soon." I motion to a large clock on the wall. "I told him to meet us here at one."

She glances past me to the wall. "It's almost one."

I nod. "You're sure this is what you want?" It's a futile question. It's all she's wanted since I told her it was her one chance to see Jenna.

"Nothing could stop me from doing this." Her eyes dash to the corner of the room.

I turn towards her gaze and see the Governor walk through the door with a small girl holding tightly to his hand. "This is it." I pull Jessica's limp hand into mine.

"There she is," she whispers softly into the air. "Look at her, Nathan. Look."

I pull my gaze from Jenna to Jessica. The grin that is covering her face is unmistakable. "You can do this," I reassure her. "You're so strong."

She nods as she looks up at me. "I can."

Chapter 25

"Jessie and Nate," Thomas calls our names as he approaches from the right. "What a coincidence."

I stare at Jessica, willing her to keep her composure. "Governor," I toss the greeting out. "What are you doing here?"

"Jessie, this is my daughter, Jenna."

Jessica moves forward and releases my hand. I feel instantly lost. I need her to help me through this as much as she needs me. "I'm Nathan," I interject even though the small girl's eyes are glued to Jessica.

"Your dress is really pretty, Jessie." She skims her small hand over the skirt. "I wish I had a dress like that."

Jessica bends over, stroking her hand over the small girl's hair. "Your dress is pretty too."

"My mommy made it for me." Her wide smile opens and the unmistakable gap of a missing tooth greets us both.

"You lost a tooth." Jessica's voice cracks and I step forward a touch to place my hand on her back. "When did you lose a tooth?"

"Last week," she says proudly. "It means I'm a big girl."

"You are a big girl." Her voice is steady and strong.

"I lost other teeth before." She points to her open mouth. "The tooth fairy came to my room three times already."

"Three times, "Jessica repeats back.

"Yes." Jenna nods slowly. "Are you my daddy's friend?"

Thomas clears his throat and I intervene as much to save Jessica from coming up with an answer, as to ward him off. "I'm your daddy's friend."

"That's cool." She reaches to grab her father's hand. "Do you like the museum?"

The question is directed at me. Her small blue eyes are glued to my face. I don't answer. I want to give Jessica every precious moment with her daughter that I can.

"We like it a lot," she answers, just as I hoped she would. "Do you like it?"

"Not so much." Jenna wrinkles her nose. "I like horses the most."

"Horses are nice." I can hear the defeat in Jessica's voice. This is too much. How could it not be? She's forced to face the child she gave up years ago.

"My mommy and daddy got me a horse." She looks up lovingly at Thomas. "I got it for my birthday."

"You're a really lucky girl." Jessica steps back and into me. I wrap my hand around her waist. "I'm glad you're so lucky."

"Me too." She bounces in place. "Can we go home now, daddy? I miss mommy."

Jessica's hand slides over mine. I feel the tremble that is racing through her.

"Let's go." Thomas pulls softly on her hand. "Say goodbye to my friends."

"Goodbye friends." She pulls her small hand to her mouth as she giggles.

My heart aches when I see it. It's what my beautiful Jessica does. We both watch in silence as Jenna walks away, holding tightly to her father's hand.

***

"I didn't make partner."

"That's fucked." She drops her purse on the small table by the door. "Who made that decision?"

"The other partners," I say before I down the rest of the bourbon I poured for myself when I got home an hour ago.

"They're fucking morons." She drops to her ass next to me.

I laugh at her words. They're actually my words. They're the very same words I've used countless times when talking about the people I work with. It's obvious that Jessica pays way more attention to what I'm complaining about than I give her credit for.

"What are you going to do now?" She asks, her hand trailing a path over my knee.

"I don't fucking know." I answer in all honesty. I wanted to act like a fucking child and pitch a fit when I got the news. If I'm being honest part of me is grateful that I wasn't chosen. It would have meant more time at the office. I would have seen even less of Jessica.

"You could wait tables at Axel," she offers. "I heard today that a few people quit so there are some openings."

"Really?" I could use the distraction of some work place gossip right now. "Why did they quit?"

"No one tells me anything." She shrugs her shoulders as she unbuttons her chef jacket. "I just heard that they are short staffed. The owner is flying in to deal with it."

"Hunter?" I question. Hunter Reynolds is the friend of a friend. I've never met the guy but I've heard a lot about him. Apparently, he's a whiz kid in the restaurant business. I may have to go down there and introduce myself once he's in town. "I should probably meet him at some point."

"You haven't met Hunter?" She tilts her head to the side.

"Not yet."

"That seems odd to me." Her lips purse together.

"Why is that odd?" I stare at my empty glass. I should get up and pour myself another. I don't have the energy for it right now.

"You know a lot of the same people he knows."

"I guess I do," I say under my breath as I watch her slide the jacket from her body revealing a plain white t-shirt. "You're not wearing a bra, Jessica."

"I know." She takes the glass from my hand and jumps to her feet. "I'll get you another. You look like you could use it."

"Why aren't you wearing a bra?"

"Sometimes it's uncomfortable when I'm working."

I take the now full glass from her hand. "You should wear a bra."

"You should lighten up." She bites on the edge of her fingernail. "Let's talk about Hunter more."

"Why?"

"I heard something else at work today." She's playful. She's hiding something from me. I recognize it in the sound of her voice. She's been sullen and withdrawn since we saw Jenna at the museum last week. I've given her the room she's needed to process that. I've let her let go in her own way and at her own pace.

"What was it?" I wish I wasn't as down as I feel. Rejection isn't a regular part of my life. Even if I wasn't completely sold on the idea of being partner, I didn't want them to reject me. This would feel a hell of a lot better if I was the one telling them that I didn't want the job.

"They're looking for a junior chef." The slight grin on her face is all the encouragement I need to snap out of my funk.

"A junior chef?" I cock a brow. "You have the qualifications for that now."

"I do." She brushes her hand across her shoulder. I can't focus. Her tits are bouncing under her thin shirt.

She stares at me in expectation. She wants me to say something that isn't related to how luscious her breasts are. How did this conversation fall so off course so fast? It's no wonder I didn't make partner. I have little focus.

"Nathan." She snaps her fingers in front of my face. "I can get the job if I want it."

"You need to take it, Jessica." I reach for her hand. "I want you to take it. I'm so proud of you."

She pulls the glass from my hand and places it on the coffee table. I want to complain. I should complain but she's so lost in her own accomplishments right now, that I can't.

"There's just one thing." The words trail over my forehead as she crawls into my lap. "It's not at Axel NY."

"What?" My hands glide over her thighs. "Where is it?"

Her hands jump to my face, tilting it up so she's staring right into my eyes. "I was going to turn it down because of the partnership."

"Fuck the partnership. I didn't get it." I inch my hands up her waist. "Where is it, Jessica?"

"We won't move unless you want to." Her lips hover next to mine. "We have to decide together."

I'll go anywhere she goes. I'd follow this woman to the farthest reaches of the earth if it meant I could wake up and look at her face every day for the rest of my life. "Tell me where it is."

"Boston." Her lips glide over mine. "Let's move to Boston."

Chapter 26

"I'm starving." I reach to grab the soft pretzel from her hand. "Why didn't we meet at a restaurant for a sandwich?"

"You told me to meet you here, Nathan." She takes a drink of lemonade from the straw. "I have to get back soon. Today is my last shift."

I nod as I look into the distance. "Give me more of that pretzel. I haven't eaten all day."

She hands the rest to me and I shove a big piece into my mouth. "Did you flirt with the pretzel guy today?" I ask before I swallow.

"I do every time I get a pretzel."

"He likes you." I wink at her and she smiles back.

"He fucking loves me." She purses her lips together before moving her hand up to push the hair away from her face.

It's windy in Central Park today. I haven't told her how much I'll miss this bench. It's a special place for me. I'm not one to drone on about sentimentality but Jessica is teaching me that small moments can offer a lot of memories. I need those. I need to start focusing on our future together.

"I should get back soon." She inches forward on the bench. "Do you want me to bring something home from the restaurant for dinner?"

I shake my head. "Not tonight. I'll cook."

She giggles loudly. I stare at her, watching as she pulls her hand to her mouth. "Nathan, you can't really cook."

"You never let me try," I counter. "I want to cook for you tonight."

"Why?"

This is it. This is the moment I've planned in my mind for weeks on end. My life is going to change the moment I do this. Everything will be different. Everything will be perfect.

Her brow furrows. "I shouldn't be late getting back. I mean they can't fire me or anything, but I don't want to screw up anything with my new job at Axel in Boston.... I don't think I ..."

I don't hear anything else she says. I can't. All I can hear is my heart pounding out a beat that is telling me to just do it. I have to do it. I turn towards her before I slide from the bench and onto my knee.

"Oh my God," she whispers the words through instant tears.

"Jessica." I look up into her face. "My beautiful, beautiful Jessica."

She nods over and over again.

I feel my own tears start. "That night at the club when you walked through the door, my entire life changed."

"Mine too," she says quietly. "Mine too."

"I told you once that the earth stopped that night so I could get on."

"I remember you saying that."

"It's the truth. I was wandering before that. I had no direction. Nothing in my life had any meaning. My heart was completely closed." My hand leaps to my chest. "I couldn't feel anything. I had no idea what love was."

She pulls the arm of her sweater over her small hand before she swipes it across her face. Her mascara paints a path across her cheek.

"You were made for me." I take in a deep, measured breath. "You were put here, on this earth, just for me. I don't doubt that. I've never doubted that."

"I know that too."

"I can't live my life without you. Half of my heart is in here." I pound my fist against my chest. "The other half is in there." I point at her chest. "You carry it with you always. Wherever you are, I'm right there within you."

"You are, Nathan." Her hand holds tightly to her chest. "You're in here with me."

"You taught me how to love you." I skim my finger over her cheek scooping up a tear. "You taught me how to love myself."

"I love you so much." She pushes her cheek into my hand.

"Jessica Roth." I reach into my suit jacket, pulling out the small blue box. "I love you more than there are stars in the sky. You are my life. You are my future. Please let me be your husband. Will you marry me?" I open the box to reveal a beautiful, emerald cut diamond ring.

Her eyes jump from mine to the ring. "Yes. I want to. Yes."
I fall into her kiss.

She pulls back slightly as her gaze darts down to the ring box. "It's the most beautiful ring in the world."

"It's your ring," I say softly. "It means you belong to me."

"I want that forever."

"Promise me it's forever, Jessica."

"Forever and always, Nathan," she whispers into my lips. "I'll never let you go."

Epilogue

A year later

"I think he looks like me." I push the blanket down to reveal his tiny chin. "He looks exactly like me."

"Nathan." Jessica reaches past me to cover Aiden back up. "You're going to wake him up."

"He's been sleeping for hours." I don't budge from my spot next to where he's resting on our bed. "He wants to play with his dad."

"He's three days old." She giggles. "He doesn't even know what playing is."

"I'll teach him." I run my hand along the small amount of black hair covering his tiny head. "I'll teach him everything."

"You're a good dad, already," Jessica whispers into my cheek. "You taught him a lot when he was still inside of me." She pats her stomach.

I stare at her beautiful body. She's next to our newborn son, resting on her side. Her body covered in a thin, pink t-shirt and matching panties. I couldn't get enough of her when she was pregnant. She told me she was expecting our son the day we got married here in Boston. It was a small ceremony. The only people at city hall with us were my parents, my sister, her husband and their two children.

"I'm really happy," I say the same words I've been telling her all day. "I can't imagine being happier than this."

"Me either." Her hand rests over mine on Aiden's forehead. "I didn't know that we'd make such a beautiful baby boy together."

"I knew," I tease. "He's parts of each of us."

"He has your hair." She jokes. "I bet he'll be just like you."

"He has your heart." I tap his tiny chest. "He'll be loving, giving and kind."

She smiles sweetly as she leans back to rest her head on the pillow. "I want him to be a good person like you are."

The words mean more than she realizes. "He will be a good person. We'll both show him how."

"You'll take him to your office when he's older?"

She's so proud of me. She tells me every day when I come home from my small office. I got a job working for the same firm I was at before I moved to New York. The place is familiar, the people are friendly and they appreciate everything I bring to the table. It's calm, it's quiet and the cases are exactly what I need. The pressure of all the Wall Street mergers and acquisitions that plagued me in New York is gone. I come home from work happy every night.

"I'll do that and you'll teach him how to cook."

"I would love to teach him that." She closes her eyes briefly. "When I'm done maternity leave, we'll figure out our schedules, right? You'll be here more and I'll work the later shift."

I love how she's worried about that now. She's on maternity leave for the next few months. "My mother and sister will help us too. They've already promised."

Watching Jessica spend time with my family has been one of the most enriching parts of our move back to Boston. She's embraced them all and they love her as family now. There's no distinction between her and I. My mother loves her as deeply as she loves me. It's what Jessica needs. It's helped her heal and feel whole again.

"I'm falling asleep." Her eyes pop open briefly. "Will you watch him sleep while I take a nap?"

"I'll be right here beside both of you." I crawl into the bed next to my wife and son. "I'll be right beside you forever."

Thank You!

Thank you for purchasing my book. I can't even begin to put to words what it means to me. If you enjoyed it, please remember to write a review for it on. Let me know your thoughts! I want to keep my readers happy.

I have more exciting books on the way, such as standalone novels and more serials, so stay tuned to my website, www.deborahbladon.com.

If you want to chat with me personally, please LIKE my page on Facebook. I love connecting with all of my readers because without you, none of this would be possible. www.facebook.com/authordeborahbladon

Thank you, for everything. xo

About the Author

Deborah Bladon has never read a romance hero she didn't like. Her love for romance novels began when she was old enough to board the bus, library card in hand to check out the newest Harlequin paperbacks. She's a Canadian by heart, and by passport, but you can often spot her in New York City sipping a latte and looking for inspiration for her next story. Manhattan is definitely her second home.

She cherishes her family and believes that each day is a gift for writing, for reading, and for loving.

4393569R00071

Printed in Germany
by Amazon Distribution
GmbH, Leipzig